W9-CBT-027

The happy couple vanished into the woods, and Braden turned to Amy.

Anger replaced grief, and even from this distance, she could see the accusation, as if she'd betrayed him somehow. The betrayal boiled down to Amy being alive while his beloved Maggie was dead.

I am in love with him.

From out of nowhere, the knowledge swept over her as powerfully as an avalanche. His expression couldn't have hurt as much as it did for any other reason. At that moment, she'd have done anything to take away his pain, even given up her life in exchange for his Maggie's if God granted her the power to make such a trade.

Her eyes held Braden's. Then, as if he couldn't bear the sight of her a moment longer, he turned away and disappeared into the trees in the opposite direction his brother and sister-in-law had gone.

MARY CONNEALY is an author, journalist, and teacher. She writes for three divisions of Barbour Publishing: Heartsong Presents, Barbour Trade Fiction, and Heartsong Presents Mysteries. Mary lives on a farm in Nebraska with her husband, Ivan. They have four daughters—Joslyn, Wendy, Shelly, and Katy—and one son-in-law, Aaron.

Don't miss out on any of our super romances. Write to us at the following address for information on our newest releases and club information.

Heartsong Presents Readers' Service
PO Box 721
Uhrichsville, OH 44683

Or visit www.heartsongpresents.com

Golden Days

Mary Connealy

Heartsong Presents

I wouldn't be writing this dedication without Cathy Marie Hake. God put her in my life.

Christy Barritt and Suzan Robertson helped make me the writer I am today.

And the Seekers are the best support group ever. They're a gift from a loving God.

A note from the Author:
I love to hear from my readers! You may correspond with me by writing:

Mary Connealy
Author Relations
PO Box 721
Uhrichsville, OH 44683

ISBN 978-1-59789-408-1

GOLDEN DAYS

Copyright © 2007 by Mary Connealy. All rights reserved. Except for use in any review, the reproduction or utilization of this work in whole or in part in any form by any electronic, mechanical, or other means, now known or hereafter invented, is forbidden without the permission of Heartsong Presents, an imprint of Barbour Publishing, Inc., PO Box 721, Uhrichsville, Ohio 44683.

All scripture quotations are taken from the King James Version of the Bible.

All of the characters and events in this book are fictitious. Any resemblance to actual persons, living or dead, or to actual events is purely coincidental.

Our mission is to publish and distribute inspirational products offering exceptional value and biblical encouragement to the masses.

PRINTED IN THE U.S.A.

one

The Alaskan Gold Rush had turned Seattle into a madhouse.

Amy Simons hurried along the noisy, teeming street. She had taken over the job of running errands for the mission because the other teachers dreaded going outside.

Amy staggered as rough, crude men shoved past, trying to move faster. The tread of booted feet and the loud shouts of gruff voices overwhelmed all other noise. Ahead, a busy street rushed with carriages and wagons. People sick with gold fever darted across. The loud lash of a whip broke through the noise. Amy glanced at an oncoming wagon drawn by four horses.

A hard shove sent her stumbling off the wooden sidewalk. Something caught her foot so she tumbled to her hands and knees into the path of the charging horses. As she fell, she heard the shouts of alarm mingled with raucous laughter.

A roar of warning from the driver barely reached her. With a shriek of terror, she threw herself out of the path of iron shod hooves. One hoof landed solidly against her side, and her head hit the hard packed ground with a sickening thud.

❧

"*Hintak xóodzi!* Papa, the hintak xóodzi! The white bear is coming!" With a deep-throated growl, a huge white bear reared up on hind legs, its claws slashing in the air.

Her father lay bleeding on the frozen ground in front of the roaring bear. He needed help. He needed her. "I will help you. I am coming, Papa."

"Amy, wake up."

The cold of artic ice bathed her face. The polar bear growled and slashed.

"Papa!" Amy swiped at the ice on her forehead. Her eyes flickered open. The dim light blinded her. Mercifully, she left the nightmare behind. An agonizing pain in her head nearly kept her from recognizing Mrs. McGraw holding a cool cloth to her forehead.

"You're safe, Amy. I'm here." The parson's wife who helped run the Child of God Mission had been mothering her since she'd arrived as a confused, grieving twelve-year-old.

Amy's eyes fell shut against throbbing pain; then she forced them open. Her stomach heaved. Mrs. McGraw became blurry, and there suddenly appeared to be two of her sitting on the bedside.

"There you are, young lady." The scolding voice echoed as if Amy heard it from across a great chasm. "Finally you've come back to us. Whatever on earth is hintak xóodzi?"

Where had Mrs. McGraw learned the Tlingit term for the great white bear? Amy hadn't spoken a word of her mother's language since she'd come south.

"It is the great white bear, a polar bear." Mother's accented English slipped from Amy's lips. Years of struggling to speak more like others in Washington State were forgotten as Amy remembered the dream of her father in danger.

"Oh, polar bears. I've heard of those. You sounded as if you were being chased by one, dear. Were you in danger from polar bears where you lived?"

"No, although they've been known to rove far from their

territory, I've never seen one. But my mother's people were nomadic and often traveled to the far north lands. I heard stories of them." The vicious, beautiful beast seemed to follow her into wakefulness, to roar and slash inside her head, or was the roaring and slashing from the pain?

Nausea twisted her stomach. She rested one hand on her belly as she fought down the urge to vomit. As Amy squinted up at the two Mrs. McGraws, one of them faded away while another remained behind, sitting at her side on the bed. Amy realized that, although the McGraws knew of her heredity, she never spoke of her mother's Tlingit tribe to anyone.

Struggling to sit up, every movement sent pain tearing through her body. Her chest blazed with an ache so deep it seemed to come from her heart. Her head pounded. Agony wracked one arm and her neck.

"Now just you stay put." Mrs. McGraw's strong, gentle hands eased Amy back. "You're going nowhere."

"But dinner. I promised to help. And I. . ." Amy tried to remember what happened. "You needed flour. I am so sorry I did not get that chore done. What happened?"

"Lie back, Amy. You were run down by a freight wagon three days ago."

"Three days?" Amy lurched upright again. The movement sent a shaft of pain through her chest and her right arm. Her left arm lashed her with pain when she moved it to clutch at her chest. Amy encountered heavy bandages wrapped tight around her ribs. She stifled a groan. "The children and the classes—I have left everything for you."

Mrs. McGraw's chubby, competent hands rested with gentle firmness on Amy's shoulders. "We've managed, child. We missed you, but we got by. Now don't fret."

Amy knew that was more than true. She wasn't needed,

but Mrs. McGraw was too kind to say so. It hadn't mattered so much when she'd been paying tuition to go to school and helping out with teaching duties. But this year, her father's tuition money hadn't come. Amy had been trying to earn her keep, but due to Mrs. McGraw's hard work and efficiency, there was little to do.

"You're battered and bruised everywhere, but nothing's broken. You just need rest and lots of it, and you'll be good as new. I'm mighty relieved you're awake, though. You've been as still as death for the most part, then restless at times as if a nightmare gripped you. We've near worn out God's ears with our prayers."

Amy forced herself to lie still, though she felt an urgency to be on her feet, caring for herself.

Mrs. McGraw carefully passed a bowl of steaming chicken soup to Amy. Amy forced her left arm to work as she took the bowl. With an encouraging pat, Mrs. McGraw left to feed the children in residence at the orphanage. Amy quit pretending to be strong. She set the spoon aside and drank the soup down using only her right hand.

The dream of her father fighting for his life haunted her. He needed her.

A few minutes later, Parson McGraw stopped by. "Awake at last, young lady? Excellent!" The parson's sparkling blue eyes, half concealed behind a shaggy head of dark hair threaded with gray, reminded Amy of her father.

"Parson, I've got to go home."

His eyebrows snapped together. "What's this? Why, Amy, home is Alaska. You don't want any part of these madmen heading north."

The newspaper called them *stampeders*, and Amy thought that described them very well. "I have to go. There has been no letter from Papa in too long. And I'm taking up space better given to the children."

"Now we've been a spell between your father's letters before. Not this long, but it's too early to worry. And there's always room in our home for you."

"I know, and I thank you for that. But Seattle has never been my home; you know that."

The parson nodded. "I've always known you'd return to the north country, but now isn't right. My heart tells me you should wait."

Wait on the Lord. The words startled her as if someone had spoken them aloud but from within. She refused to be deterred. "I am going. I have to."

Parson McGraw's eyes softened, and his kind expression grew serious. "This morning during my Bible-reading time I found a verse that seems very appropriate to this moment. In fact, I'm wondering if God didn't guide my hand to select those pages and that passage."

"What passage is that?"

"It's from Isaiah. It says, 'They that wait upon the Lord shall renew their strength; they shall mount up with wings as eagles; they shall run, and not be weary; and they shall walk, and not faint.' The verse touched me because we'd been so worried about you, and those words encouraged me greatly. But now I'm wondering if God didn't lead me to them for you as much as for me."

Amy swallowed, fighting to keep her determination strong in the face of the parson's gentle wisdom.

"I have such a powerful desire to go home, Parson. I cannot stay here knowing Papa has tarried so long with his letter. He may be in danger. I have to go see."

He tried to dissuade her. Later his wife took her turn. Amy

slept poorly that night, awakening in pain every time she shifted in bed, haunted by nightmares when she did slumber.

And under the pain and the nightmares, both awake and asleep, whispered a voice that said, *Wait*.

Perhaps the Lord himself urged her to accept the generosity of these kind people. But rest went against her nature, and taking charity hurt her independent spirit nearly as badly as the bruises hurt her body.

She wanted the midnight sun.

She wanted the vast, rugged beauty of her home.

She wanted Alaska.

two

April 14, 1898
On board the steamship Northward
on the Inside Passage to Alaska

A thick-soled boot nearly landed on her drawn-in toes. "Miss?"

Amy jumped at the gravelly voice. Her ribs punished her for the sudden movement.

The man crouched beside her, entering her line of vision as she looked up. Worry cut lines between his dark red brows. "I noticed you didn't eat."

She twisted awkwardly to face him and gasped as pain stabbed her.

"Are you all right?" His hair shone red, longish and neglected like her father's. Unruly curls blew in the salt-water breeze.

His skin was fair, his cheeks chapped by the cold spring air. His face bore the stubble of their week-long passage on the ship. Between the rolling of the ship and the absence of hot water, shaving was impossible. One large freckled hand with clean, blunt fingers, held a plate full of what passed for food on this wretched ship. The bracing wind had banished any aroma of the plate of beans. Just as well. The aroma amounted to a stench.

She didn't answer his question. Admitting how weak she felt put her at a disadvantage. She knew too well the ways of the wild where a wounded member of a herd faced the destiny of being picked out by the wolves. For pure survival, she forced herself to eat once a day, but she preferred hunger to the mob scene in the galley.

Amy looked at the man's shining blue eyes and felt as if she could see the wide Alaskan sky. She was tempted to search their depths until she saw home. As she looked closer, she saw that something dimmed the glow. He seemed to bear some weight that surrounded and smothered him. The missionaries had spoken sternly of proper behavior, but nothing about this man seemed dangerous.

"Thank you. That is very kind." She reached a hand toward the plate and nearly snatched it back when she saw how it trembled. She didn't think of herself as weak, but her hand told a different story. She didn't like her weakness revealed to this stranger.

He handed the plate over along with a fork, then turned and settled on the deck beside her. "This is a nice spot. I hope you don't mind my intruding."

She noticed he shifted around until his body blocked the wind for her—another kindness. "No, of course not. It is so close inside. I needed some fresh air."

"Close, huh? A nice word for people packed like sardines into the belly of a converted freighter with no windows, no baths, and no manners." He turned to look at her as she scooped up the first bite.

She smiled at the Irish lilt in his voice.

"Name's Braden Rafferty. It's a sad day when a little lady like you sets off with a boatful of madmen on the hunt for a pot o' gold."

Amy grinned. "I am Amy Simons." *Amaruq Simonovich.* She was tempted to tell him her real name. Papa had thought she'd be treated better with a more American name, and she'd respected his wishes.

"My father is in Alaska close to the area where they found gold. I am forced to accompany seven hundred madmen north." She flinched and turned, mindful of her ribs. "I am sorry. I did not mean to imply you are a madman."

She glanced sideways. Braden smiled. The smile broke slowly across his face. It seemed at odds with the downward furrows around his mouth as if his natural expression was always sad. And the smile didn't reach his eyes—as if no amount of amusement could touch him. But for all of that, it was a nice smile.

"In my own way I reckon I *am* a madman. I'm joining my brother. He's got a claim north of Skaguay. He didn't go all the way into the Klondike. Some old trapper convinced him he'd find all the gold he wanted far closer to civilization."

Some old trapper made Amy think of her father.

"Not sure if he's found any. He didn't send much money home to buy supplies. But he has found himself a wife, built a cabin, and sounds content." Braden's smile faded. "Now here I am, leaving a prosperous farm and my parents, who need me. That's madness, I reckon."

Amy scooped up more food, only now realizing how hungry she'd become. She did her best not to taste the bland, mushy mess, but she felt steadier as her stomach filled.

"So, you're going with this hoard to Dawson's Creek, is that right?" Braden settled against the bulkhead as Amy scraped the last bite of food off her plate.

Shaking her head, she swallowed. "I am taking this ship to Sitka, then on to Skaguay. From there, I will hike up the Skaguay River to my father's cabin. He is deep enough in the wilderness as it is. No need to tramp another five hundred miles." Amy heard her voice taking on the sound of her mother. More and more since the accident two weeks ago, she'd found herself reverting to the heavily accented English she'd learned from her Tlingit mother and Russian father. She liked the sound of the broader vowels and the simplicity of speaking without contractions.

Braden sat up straighter and faced her. "I disembark in Skaguay, too. If you're familiar with the land, maybe you could look at the directions my brother sent." Braden reached inside the patch pocket of his buckskin jacket.

Another man stepped in front of them. His body blocked the few pale rays of sun. Annoyed, Amy looked up.

A stocky, middle-aged man in ill-fitting work clothes dropped to his knees on the deck squarely in front of her. With the constant flow of miners at his back, he crowded too close to Amy. Then he smiled at her in a way that reminded her that her name *Amaruq* meant wolf.

"Mind if I steal a bit o' space out'a the wind, folks?"

Since the deck wasn't hers to give or take, Amy didn't see how she could say no. She did notice that the man wasn't out of the wind. He looked blue-lipped and miserable. No light of fanatic gold fever shone in his eyes. Amy glanced at the man's hands—soft city hands. Lots of city folks had thrown in on the hunt for gold, but you could read the hunger in their eyes. Why would this man be going north if not driven by that same hunger?

"Name's Barnabas Stucky, miss. I see you're travelin' alone. Y'ever need any help, you ask for Barnabas, and I'll come'a runnin'."

Barnabas Stucky struck her as more dangerous than most men, and she trusted her instincts.

The fur traders she'd grown up with came in all kinds. Although with her Russian blood, Amy didn't have coloring or skin as dark as most Tlingits, when she was with her mother, she had faced occasional prejudice. She'd met those who would be kind to a Tlingit child, those that would avoid a child out of awkwardness, and those who were dangerous to anyone, child or adult. Stucky fit with the latter group.

"Thank you, sir. I am fine, but I will remember your offer." She looked away, hoping the man would leave.

Braden took the plate from Amy. Amy glanced at him, then sideways at Mr. Stucky. Stucky's eyes narrowed. He took a hard look at Braden, making obvious motions for him to leave. Stucky's eyes sharpened as if eager to be alone with Amy.

She grabbed Braden's hand.

three

"We were going to discuss the way to your brother's cabin, I believe?" Amy's hand dug into Braden's wrist even through the buckskin.

He heard the soft cry for help in her question. Her quiet voice, with the echo of some nearly forgotten accent, stopped him from returning the plate to the galley.

Braden looked from her unexpected touch to her wary eyes. He relaxed back against the steel wall behind him. Of course it had to do with the city slicker. Braden hadn't liked the looks of him, either. She'd chosen him to protect her.

"You're my strength, Braden."

Maggie's voice haunted him every waking minute. He'd been a protector before and done a poor enough job of it. If he had any sense, he'd run and leave this foolish little woman to fend for herself. She appeared ill equipped for the rugged life of Alaska. Frail and withdrawn, too thin, too pale, afraid of her own shadow, she didn't even have the sense to feed herself. Easing his shoulders flat against the wall, Braden admitted her reasons didn't matter. She wanted him to stay—he'd stay.

A heavy, black braid rested over her shoulder and reached down long enough to curl in at her feet in front of her drawn-up knees. Her eyes, black as midnight, were pretty, but her lids looked heavy, as if she were near collapse. She had a faint upward slant to her eyes and a dark complexion, lightened by the pallor of a woman who avoided the outdoors, like his Maggie had. Even with her father there to protect her, any

16

fool could see she wouldn't survive an Alaskan winter.

Braden clenched his jaw to keep from telling her just that. Instead, he settled in close and pulled Ian's letter out of the pocket of his heavy, well-lined buckskin coat. Then he began to pick up the conversation they'd been having before Stucky's interruption.

"My brother and his wife live upstream, east of Skaguay." Braden extended the letter to Amy.

She smoothed back the sheet of white paper. Its crinkle sounded civilized against the huffing of the steam engine and the rough voices and clomping feet of the passing men.

Stucky leaned forward, as if trying to sneak a peek at the letter. Braden couldn't imagine why unless he thought they had a treasure map leading straight to a mountain of pure gold. Well, let the man look. He'd soon see it was no such thing.

Amy jerked her chin up, and her huge, dark eyes lit with interest. "This is very close to where my father lives. I will be going this way out of Skaguay. I can guide you."

Braden stifled a sigh. Aye, and he could do all the work so she didn't get her lily white hands dirty and carry her so she didn't stub her toe. Dandy. "Sure, we can travel together. I'll see you to your da's house; then you can get me headed in the right direction for my brother's claim."

Amy smiled, her straight white teeth shining. She looked little all over, more than half a foot shorter than his six feet one, with fine-boned hands, and a stubborn chin under that pretty smile.

For a second, Braden forgot what a burden she would be. But then he remembered Maggie's smile and knew what lay ahead. With a sigh, he swallowed his irritation. Sure, and he'd deliver the lass to her father because it was his Christian duty.

And he'd use the burdensome chore as a reminder, every step of the way, that a man paid too great a price for trying to be someone else's strength.

❧

Someone walked her way on the deck in the dark. Amy'd expected him to come. With a twinge of shame, she thought of how weak she'd been since the accident. But despite her shame, pleasure stole into her heart and raised her spirits. She looked up to see Braden with a plate of those awful beans.

He crouched beside her and handed her the plate, then scooted around to block the wind with his broad shoulders.

"You did not need to do this, Mr. Rafferty." Amy scooped the first bite in her mouth, feeling as if she'd been given a gift.

"It isn't right for you to fight your way though that rabble." Braden pulled his hat low over his eyes. "Although, I 'spect I qualify as rabble myself."

Amy grinned as she chewed the bland meal.

His eyes were shaded by his hat, but he must have seen her smile because one shoulder hunched.

She swallowed. "The wind is kind tonight. You do not have to shelter me. Go ahead and rest your back against the wall."

Turning her attention back to the plate, she ate quietly for a while before he finally slid down to sit on the deck.

As they sat there in the full dark, a long, thin ray of green light climbed in the sky. Amy sighed.

"Sure and the sunset is giving us quite a painting to watch tonight," Braden said, easing his shoulders and shifting a bit so there was only an inch between them.

The lilt to his voice was pleasant to Amy's ears. "It is not the sunset. That is past. Rather it is *gis'óok.*"

"What?" Braden lifted his hat with his thumb.

"Uh, I mean it is the Northern Lights, a miraculous moving

night sky." Feeling as though she were a liar, Amy didn't explain the native words she'd learned from her mother's people. She knew Braden wouldn't care that she was of another nationality than he. Or did she? Father had seemed so sure her Tlingit and Russian blood would set her apart. Being set apart from the gold-seeking madmen would be glorious. She clenched her jaw to keep from speaking about the Tlingit legends surrounding the gis'óok.

Braden sat up straight. "I've heard of these lights. This is the first night I've come out on deck after dark. It seems like the night drives a man to bed. But I saw you'd missed the meal again, so I came up here lookin' for you."

Amy turned away from the growing light show and smiled. "Thank you."

He tipped his hat at the sky. "That's the Northern Lights, heh?"

"It is said that you can see them in Seattle, but where I lived in the city there were street lights, and many children to put to bed at the time I would normally gaze at the sky."

"Where's that?"

"The Child of God Mission." A streak of red slowly lifted alongside the green. "Ah, God hangs a curtain of crimson beside the green tonight. Far more often it is shades of green and white. The color of flame is a rare gift."

Braden stiffened a bit, and Amy wondered if she'd said something wrong. She chose to be still rather than make it worse.

"So you think God goes to the bother of giving us pretty colors in the night sky, do you?"

Amy nearly flinched at his bitterness. Unsure how to answer, she silently watched the colors climb and fade, new ones following old, each a different color, some bright, some so faint they were barely visible.

The lights soothed her soul. At last, into the glorious, colorful darkness, Amy said, "I think God set the world into motion. He made the dark and the light, the rain and the clear sky. I believe in Jesus to protect my soul but I think God expects me to use the intelligence He gave me to protect my life. He lets the world work as it would, and He gives us the sense and strength to survive in it."

"Or not survive."

"I cannot argue with what you say. There was no one stronger than my mother. No one more equipped to handle the rugged land and more wise in its ways. And still, she fell on a narrow trail crossing one of her beloved mountains and broke her leg. She, who had never been sick, caught the fever and died. So yes, some don't survive."

"How long ago did she die?"

Amy turned and saw that Braden watched her, not the sky. "I was twelve summers. I wanted to stay and care for my father and stay in my land. But Papa would not hear of it. He needed to be gone for long weeks in the winter, running his trap lines, collecting the furs that supported us. He said the loneliness of our remote cabin would drive me mad—if it did not kill me."

Braden nodded. "Your father sounds like a wise man."

"He said it was the most painful thing he had ever lived through save the death of my mother. At the time, I only saw it as losing the only person alive whom I loved." Amy looked away from Braden to watch the sky and hide tears. "If my grandfather had still lived, he would have come. Together, we might have been able to convince Papa to let me stay. But Grandfather had died by then. When I left, I felt torn away from life as surely as if my heart had been ripped out of my chest."

Silence settled, and Amy decided Braden would say no more to her.

Just as she'd have turned away to watch the sky, he said, "I'm sorry. I'm so sorry that happened to you, Amy."

The mystical lights rained down from above. Their eyes met. An eternity stretched between them.

Braden leaned toward her for one confusing, exciting moment. A feeling Amy didn't understand stirred in her chest. Then he jerked back, his expression suddenly as cold as the icebergs that lined the passage through which they traveled.

Braden turned away, his shoulder hitting the wall behind them with a dull thud. Amy didn't know what to say or do.

Wait on the Lord.

This once, the whisper touched her, and she savored the closeness to God, glad that she wasn't completely alone in the world. Braden by her side, so distant and quiet, reminded her of just how alone she was. She turned back to her plate and finished the beans quickly, ignoring the spectacular night sky, dim compared to the rainbow of pain arcing across her heart.

The moment Amy had cleaned her plate, Braden took it from her and rose. "I'll find you here in the morning then." He walked away quickly, leaving her so alone that the deck took on a menacing feel.

Sitting in her dark, lonely place, she felt the push of fear telling her to go in where there were people. For once, the echoes of God's guidance weren't urging her to wait.

She heard a muffled footfall in the direction opposite of the one Braden had gone. Instinct drove her to her feet. Her ribs protested the sudden movement, but she didn't tarry. She scurried down to the putrid little cabin full of bunks stacked three high, a room she shared with so many others.

For once, instead of smothering her, the close quarters offered protection.

Unable to sleep because of the early hour, Amy was glad the cabin window stood open, offering a bit of fresh air that only partially dispelled the miasma of sickness and filth. She watched out that tiny open circle and enjoyed the curtain of light until she fell into a fitful sleep. Footfalls chased her in her dreams, a pursuit that lasted throughout the night.

ɤ

Faithfully, Braden brought Amy three meals a day, and they ate together on the cold deck. Amy had never spent time with a young man before, and she found she enjoyed visiting with him. They talked of many things, though she noticed he never spoke of his past.

By the time the *Northward* arrived in Skaguay, Amy's ribs didn't stab her quite as often. Fatigue still plagued her. *Why didn't I stay at the mission and heal for a few more weeks?*

She'd have been welcome. She even knew God wanted her to take time to rest. But that knowledge hadn't seemed important. Home would renew her strength, although getting there might well kill her. She had no strength yet, and a long journey lay ahead of her.

The Skaguay dock, from which she'd departed nearly six years ago, shocked her. The sleepy little village of a dozen houses and more dogs than people had turned into a boom-town. Ships lined the narrow pier. The creak of ropes and pulleys off-loading supplies from various vessels blotted out the serene voice of the wilderness. Skaguay loomed ahead of her like an ugly sore on the pristine land.

Amy leaned on the railing along with as many stampeders as could fight their way forward. Ignoring the unwashed bodies and rough voices that surrounded her, she fought back tears at the destruction of her beautiful Alaska.

She thought of her mother. Harmony had existed between Yéil Simonovich and the wilderness. Alaska, a land of abundant food and fuel, its beauty stretching so high and wide it seemed eternal, looked like an extension of heaven. The territory stretched in all directions so vast Amy had believed everyone could come, and there would still be room for more.

She was wrong. It was ruined.

Touching a hand to her trembling lips, Amy watched in silence as the *Northward* inched its way to the dock. The stampeders surged forward, jostling Amy, making her grateful for her nearly healed ribs. A heavy hand seemed to settle on her back, although she felt certain the touch wasn't personal. For an instant, Amy remembered that busy Seattle street and the careless shoving hands accompanied by cruel laughter that had sent her tumbling into the path of a carriage.

Amy grabbed the waist-high railing. A fall over the side would be fatal with the distance to plummet and the heavy drag of the *Northward* pulling water beneath it as it inched along. Amy turned sideways, determined to force her way back from the rail.

She looked up into the eyes of a man she'd caught watching her from a distance several times. That alone didn't surprise her. A lot of men watched her. They watched all the women. But this one's eyes had been sharper than most, with something in them different than that male gleam a woman came to recognize.

Had he been the one pushing on her? A shudder began deep inside as she thought of the long fall to certain death.

"Miss Simons?" The man touched the brim of his slouching brown hat. It might have been a cowboy hat at one time, but it had been battered until it sagged over his ears and only curved in the crown because his head held it in place. He seemed to be shoved forward at the mercy of the pack.

He had a saddle bag over one shoulder with a flat seining pan clattering softly against a pick anytime the ship bobbed or the shifting mass of humanity bumped him.

Keeping a firm grip on the railing, she said, "Yes?" She didn't like him knowing her name, although she imagined few secrets remained about her after all this time aboard ship. Her wariness didn't ease just because he had a few manners.

"My name is Thompson, Miss Simons, Darnell Thompson. I couldn't help overhearing you discuss your journey with Braden Rafferty." The man smiled, but to Amy his expression seemed calculating.

He shrugged under his shearling coat. "I'm headed in much the same direction myself. I wondered if I might travel along with you once we leave the ship."

Amy couldn't bring herself to casually include him. "Whether we travel the same trail or not is surely not my decision."

The man watched her. Looking around for a long moment, his eyes focused over her shoulder as if he saw someone he knew. He gave one firm nod. "Fair enough. More men on a trail makes for safe passage. I'll discuss it with Rafferty."

"You do that." Amy stared into the man's eyes. They were a strange hazel color, brown flecked with gold. The mission teacher had taught her to be wary of men, and though she'd made an exception for Braden, this man didn't inspire such trust.

Mr. Thompson tugged on his much-maligned hat and left her by the railing. Although he'd looked past Amy's shoulder at someone or something, he turned and went in the opposite direction. Seconds later, Stucky appeared at her back.

Amy clenched her jaw, preparing to use all the cool manners she'd learned from the missionaries. Before she had to bear the miner's questions, Braden approached. Amy glanced around, expecting Thompson to come up again and invite himself on the trail. He'd melted into the crowd even though moving through this mob seemed nearly impossible.

She tried to spot Thompson so she could point him out to Braden.

He was gone.

four

He was gone!

Braden pushed roughly past the men that separated him from Amy. Complaints and return shoves didn't stop him. Where had that man gone? Their eyes had met for just a second, and Braden hadn't liked what he'd seen.

As Braden reached Amy's side, he breathed more easily. "One of the crew members said we should be able to hop off this crate in an hour. Standing by the railing won't get you off a second faster." Without mentioning the man who'd taken off, Braden caught her arm.

Now past the grumbling men, Braden noticed that worthless Barnabas Stucky standing at Amy's elbow—another overly interested miner.

Amy's eyes widened at his firm grip, but Braden felt an urgent need to get her out of this crush. He nodded at Stucky, then parted the throng of stampeders, dragging Amy away from the edge. Since the men were all trying to get closer to the railing, they let Braden pass with little trouble.

Braden worked his way around the ship. The side not facing port was nearly deserted, and he leaned against the wall. He'd seen that Amy had her meals here every morning, noon, and night since that first time he'd brought her food. The ship served no breakfast this morning because the crew had been occupied since before dawn with navigating the Skaguay port. But they'd dock early so they'd find a meal on shore.

Disgusted with Amy's lack of survival skills, Braden wondered if she'd have even lived through the trip without his help. He leaned against the wooden walls of the wheel house and crossed his arms. "We'll just wait here until the captain tells us to disembark."

"Thank you for helping me through that mob." Amy spoke quietly as she always did. Her voice carried a note of calm, a husky sweet sound that soothed his battered heart. She leaned beside him, one arm wrapped around her chest, staring straight forward at the mountains across the bay from Skaguay.

Through the entire voyage she favored her side, although in their long days together on the boat, she'd never mentioned being hurt. Of course, Braden hadn't talked about himself much, either. They'd discussed the trek to Ian's house and the rough voyage and the conditions Braden could expect in Alaska, but he'd never so much as said Maggie's name.

Maggie would have shared every trouble. Amy's lack of complaint told Braden she wasn't hurt, just weak, probably stiff and sore from the rugged voyage. She never should have taken this trip.

"Welcome." Braden nodded and stared at the majesty of Alaska looming high over the ship. When the beauty of the mountains had worked its way into his soul, he produced his letter from Ian one more time and discussed the route with Amy until long after the ship had docked and the deck had cleared.

Amy overflowed with ideas for the journey home, and Braden found it easy to trust her.

❧

"I don't trust him." Braden whispered to Amy.

The gaunt, bearded man to whom Amy had led him limped away.

"Why'd you pick this man to haul my supplies?" Braden watched the man, looking more animal than human, scratch his neck as he hobbled along. His long, snarled hair, black and streaked with gray, straggled below a fur hat with dangling ear covers.

"Wily? He has been carting supplies up the river all my life. He will do fine by us." Amy barely glanced at Braden, then followed after the foul-smelling man.

Braden suspected the man had been avoiding baths all his life.

The man snagged his suspenders with his thumbs from where they drooped around his hips and snapped them over his shoulders. Then he stooped over, grabbed a pair of ropes off the ground that were attached to an oddly shaped boat, and began pulling the strange contraption down the bank toward the vast bay that opened on the south side of the settlement of Goose Chase.

Amy got on the uphill side of the thing. It looked like a flat boat wrapped in animal hide. She dropped to her knees in the sand with a groan Braden heard from ten feet away, and began shoving. Braden looked at his sizable stack of supplies, which he'd transported from the ship to Goose Chase by paying an outrageous sum to rent a rickety hand cart.

Amy shoved, and Braden decided that even if it meant letting someone steal everything he'd brought for Ian, even his mother's precious mantel clock, he couldn't let Amy do hard labor she was obviously unsuited for.

He moved to her side. "What is this thing?"

Amy looked up from her position on her knees. "It is an *umiak.*"

"What?"

"It is a boat called an umiak. It has a wooden frame, and

Wily has his covered with walrus hide. It is suited for shallow water and heavy loads."

Braden thought about it and figured if a walrus wasn't waterproof then nothing was. His supplies—six good-sized boxes—would nearly fill it. Good thing Amy didn't seem to have anything beyond the small satchel she slung over her neck and shoulder. Just more evidence of how ill-equipped she was for this journey.

"Let me do that." He dropped on his knees beside her and gave his head a little sideways jerk to get her out of the way.

With a grateful smile, Amy got to her feet and let him take over. Between him and Wily, they had the boat launched in a couple of minutes. Wily pulled the floating umiak down the bay toward Braden's supplies.

Braden and Wily worked in silence loading. Wily looked up at Amy and asked, "Ride, little Amaruq?"

Braden tried to figure out just what he'd heard. *Amaruq?* The man slurred his words like he almost never used his voice, which Braden could believe considering how little he'd spoken so far.

"Until you hit the current." Amy nodded. "Then I'll walk." She climbed in.

Braden noticed the lack of room for him in the umiak. He didn't get a chance to ask where he was supposed to sit before Wily began leading the boat up the bay, away from Goose Chase and civilization.

Amy and Wily were about twenty feet away from him before Braden realized he was walking, no doubt all the way to Ian's camp, over twenty miles away through some of the roughest territory in the world. The steamship had docked early, and they'd walked the miles to Goose Chase as quickly as possible, towing the cart. The trip could be made in one day easily in the normal course of things. Then Braden looked ahead at the big, blue water of the bay. It narrowed in the distance and cut between two mountains that sprang straight up from the water's edge. How were they supposed to walk through that?

A rustling of bushes behind them reminded Braden of the men who had shown interest in accompanying them. It made no sense. The stampeders headed up the Chilkoot Pass toward Dawson's Creek. Why would a gold-hungry miner want to follow them? Braden had turned down an offer of company from Stucky and that sharp-eyed stranger named Thompson, who'd hovered too close to Amy on the boat. Neither had seemed as interested in the gold as they were in Amy.

Braden had done his best to lose them in the horde at the dock, even though they had to tug along the cart Amy had found. They'd headed out of Skaguay, walking down what looked like a game trail to Goose Chase. He'd thought they'd slipped away unnoticed. Now those rustling bushes made him wonder.

Should he investigate? He studied the undergrowth, then looked forward toward the mountain Wily seemed determined to walk over. Braden forgot the bushes and trudged forward, filled with dread.

⁓

Filled with wonder, Amy leaned forward, so eager to get through the bay and into the narrow waters of the Skaguay River that she could barely stay seated. Hearing her Tlingit name for the first time in years renewed her spirit. She'd known Wily from her earliest memory.

The beauty was so profound Amy wondered if God had created Alaska as a drink for a thirsty soul. She longed to get out of Wily's slow-moving umiak and march away from this easy water passage and into her wilderness. She stayed put, of course. She was in a hurry to get to Papa. Now wasn't the time to reacquaint herself with her magnificent home. And she knew there'd be no riding when Wily's umiak started scraping along the bottom of the river. They'd need every hand on the ropes. With her ribs still aching, she did the practical thing and saved her energy. Alaska, by dint of trying to kill everyone who came here, taught a person to be practical.

Amy looked at the contents of the umiak behind her and wondered what pile of impractical frippery Braden Rafferty hauled in those crates. It was just more evidence of how ill-equipped he was for this journey.

Amy had a single change of clothes, her knife, a cloth book of needles, and a small, cast-iron skillet. The indulgence of the skillet nearly shamed her, and Amy hoped Wily never found out about it. He'd shake his head as he had so many times when, as a child, she'd shown fascination with the things Wily hauled. He didn't talk much, but he'd let her know she'd gone soft.

She could easily enough create a pan out of a soaked slab of bark from a cedar tree. Her mother had raised her right. The cedar even added a nice flavor. But a skillet worked better and took less tending. With her sore ribs and aching muscles, she'd been inclined to spoil herself. When she'd sold off her things to pay for the trip home, she found a few coins to spare for a frying pan in case she ended up camping along the trail. But there'd be no camping. Because of the early docking of the ship, she'd be home in a single day.

Of course, some of Braden's things would be supplies. And Amy wasn't innocent of indulging her papa. She'd sent a bit of sugar and a few pounds of flour to him every spring, even though he only asked for traps or tools.

Amy sighed, wondering where Papa had gotten to. Her stomach twisted. Why hadn't he written? He was an old man by her Tlingit people's standards, nearly forty. He might not be tough enough to tackle Alaskan winters and survive all this territory threw at him. She wished suddenly that she'd had the money to bring her papa a few treats. Perhaps she shouldn't fault Braden for toting foolish things over a mountain.

"Can I help pull?" Braden's voice turned her to face the shore. He held out a hand for one of the two ropes Wily had slung over his shoulder. Wordlessly, Wily handed one over. She watched Braden loop the rope until it was a bit shorter. Braden fell in, following a few steps behind Wily. The going was easy now, but the terrain ahead would be rough.

She couldn't wait to get into the mountains. As she drank in their beauty, she realized that away from these mountains she'd only been half alive.

≈

This mountain wanted him dead.

Braden's foot slipped off a rock, and he sank to his ankle in the icy river. The weather was mild, but the water still held the frigidity of winter within it. Wily had given him a pair of waterproof boots. Amy told him they were made of walrus intestines so his feet stayed dry—bitterly cold, but dry. The spring thaw allowed them to pass, but ice patches still lined the river, and in places, the umiak had to break through a thin sheet of stubborn spring ice. They'd been going at a forced march since they docked at Skaguay this morning, and Amy had assured him he'd sleep at Ian's tonight.

Enjoying the motion that stretched his muscles, long inactive on the boat, wouldn't have been so bad if his feet weren't frozen lumps.

"Papa's cabin is just ahead." Amy eased the rope off her shoulder and straightened.

Braden watched her for signs of collapse. She'd worked hard once the water got shallow and they'd crossed to the other side of the river, throwing her shoulder into the rope. Braden had protested, sure Amy would collapse within a mile, but Wily and Amy overruled him. Wily handed over the rope to Amy, then waded behind the umiak, pushing it over the sand when it bottomed out. Braden had insisted on taking the lead rope, pulling for all he was worth to keep Amy's work to a minimum.

They'd started as quickly as they could get off the ship and get to Goose Chase and had been dragging this blasted umiak—or whatever Amy called it—for hours.

Braden's shoulder ached. The fabric of his shirt was tattered. He'd shed his coat long ago.

Amy sighed so loudly Braden stopped. He looked back to see if she was in danger and saw a huge grin on her normally somber face. Her white teeth flashed.

"We are here." She faced the woods.

"Your father's cabin is near here?" Braden looked at the steeply pitched, heavily wooded area. Amy was visibly exhausted. Even smiling, she had dark circles under her eyes, and despite the brisk spring air, her face had an unnatural pallor.

"No, it *is* here." Amy pointed into the forest. Suddenly it popped out at him. A cabin sat about one hundred feet back into the woods. The place blended completely with the rough-and-tumble woods.

Braden noticed they were out of the wind and no snow lay on the ground around the cabin. A shaft of sunlight shone down through a gap and shared its generous warmth with the house. A man wise in the ways of the wilderness had chosen this spot. With a sigh of relief, Braden knew that despite the odd, tumbled-down look of the cabin, the man inside possessed wood smarts and would keep his daughter safe.

Braden looked at Amy. She glowed.

"Let's go say hello. Then you can point me toward my brother's place."

Amy nodded, but then her eyes narrowed, and the bright smile faded from her face.

"Your brother's on up the stream a piece." Wily's voice sounded farther away than it should be. "I'm gonna keep headin' up."

Braden heard the faint scrape of the bottom of the umiak on the rocky river bottom and turned to see Wily moving along.

"Something is wrong." Amy strode toward the cabin.

As Braden hurried after her, he realized that there was more to this house than he'd first thought. A second room had been built on at an angle. The roof sloped sharply upward, most likely to keep the snow from piling up, but it looked sizable enough for a loft.

Dark furs hung on the front, a long one that must cover the front door and two smaller ones that could only be windows. Patches of cedar bark and branches made it resemble a stack of trees blown into a pile by the wind.

"I can see something's wrong. It's been damaged." Braden decided he'd help with the repairs.

"No, it always looks like this."

"The windows have always been broken out?"

"No, we have always covered the windows with furs." Amy arched an eyebrow at him as if he'd said something ridiculous. "Where would a person get glass?" She hurried on.

Braden stayed at her side. "Then what's wrong with the place?" By the look on her face, he knew whatever bothered her was serious.

"There is smoke coming out of the chimney." Amy's breath sounded labored as she quickened her pace.

That's a silly reason to get so upset. "Maybe your da needed to heat the place up. Maybe he's cooking."

"Papa? Need heat or cook inside? This late in the spring?" Amy began running toward the house.

five

The journey up river had almost finished Amy. She'd used every ounce of her strength, tapping deep inside for the courage to go on, knowing she would soon rest in Papa's house.

As she rushed toward her home, a whisper on the wind, one she didn't care to heed, told her to wait on the Lord. She'd heard this ever since she'd awakened after the accident in Seattle, determined to leave the city, but she'd ignored it. Yes, God might be trying to make things easy for her, but she didn't need easy. She could take care of herself.

Her legs wobbled as she forced them forward. Her ribs punished her for running. She clutched them to quiet the pain and held herself erect by sheer will. It shamed her to rely on someone else. She should have been able to take care of herself.

Shaking off her fear, Amy reached for the grizzly pelt that kept the wind out of the cracks in the door.

She hesitated, remembering her manners learned from the McGraws. It was home; she should just go on in. But she'd been gone so long. She stood on the slab of gray rock centered in front of the door and knocked, her fist muffled by the bear skin and the rugged door frame. No one came to the door, and her jaw tightened with impatience as the moment stretched. Why had Papa stopped writing? Why had he worried her like this for so long?

"Amy, maybe we should—"

"Should what, Braden?" She whirled to face him. "I am

home. This is the end of my journey. There is nowhere else for me to go."

No one answered her knock on the log framing the door, so she pulled back the pelt and shoved on the door. It was firmly latched. Papa hadn't even had a latch on the door while she lived here!

Her fear was too much to face, so she grabbed hold of a flicker of annoyance and turned it to anger. Pounding on the door, she glanced up at the smoking chimney. Someone was here but not Papa. He wouldn't abide stifling smoke when he could breathe the pure Alaskan air.

If he was here, he must be sick. If Papa couldn't come to the door, then she'd beat the door down and go in uninvited.

"Papa, it is Amy! Open this door!" She hammered with the side of her fist on the saplings that had been lashed together into a tidy door, heavy enough to keep out the winter wind and a pack of hungry wolves.

Suddenly it flew open. Braden caught her before she fell into the arms of a stranger. The man who stood before her was certainly not her father.

"I dunno an Amy. Beat it!"

The door began to swing shut. Amy threw herself forward and blocked it open. Her ribs hurt from the impact. On a gasp of pain, her vision blurred. "What are you doing here? Where is my father?"

The man's eyes narrowed, lost in a full beard and coarse, knotted hair. He sneered at her. Teeth bared green and broken. "No father in this place. Now git!"

Amy spoke quickly. "My papa, Petro. . .Peter Simons owns this cabin. Tell me where he is."

The man quit sneering. He quit trying to get his door shut. His eyes were suddenly cold, and he studied her intently. A vile smell rolled off the man and out of the cabin. When Amy had lived here, the cabin had a clean, woodsy aroma.

"No need to get riled, mister." Braden shifted slightly so his shoulder blocked the man who had invaded Amy's home.

The man's conniving eyes slid toward Braden, and with a little clutch of her heart, Amy knew only Braden's presence kept her safe. That whispering voice had warned her. God knew of the danger. But Braden *was* here, although it galled her that she needed him.

"Pete Simons din't have no kin. He lived alone long'ez I knew him. And he never made no mention of any daughter. No woman is gonna come in here layin' claim to what's rightfully mine."

"Yours?" Amy's temper built until she was too upset to be afraid. "That is a lie! It belongs to Peter Simons."

"It did 'til he sold it to me."

Amy gasped. "Papa sold the cabin?"

"Sure as shootin' he did. Got me a bill of sale'n ever'thin'." The man looked her up and down in a way that made her skin crawl. "An' I knew Pete for years. Never heard him talk of a daughter. Who put you up to makin' a claim to my place?"

Her father loved this cabin. He wouldn't have sold it because he didn't see it as belonging to him. Her father had been deeded this place by an old Russian friend. Papa loved his rugged life and carved out a home here. No bill of sale would convince her differently.

Then Amy thought past all her anger. "Where is my father? If he sold you the cabin, then he must have moved on somewhere else. Tell me where he is."

The man crossed his arms. "You expect me to believe you're Pete's daughter 'n you don't know he's dead?"

Amy gasped. "No! No, I do not believe you. I would have heard!"

Amy backed away from the awful words. Braden slipped a strong arm around her waist.

"I don't b'lieve you're his daughter. You're on my property, and I want you off. The next time you hammer on my door, I won't come unarmed." The man glanced again at Braden, then turned his cruel gaze on her.

Amy shuddered to think what might have happened if she'd come here alone.

The man gave her one last wild glare, then stepped back and slammed the door in her face.

A cry ripped out of Amy's throat, and she launched herself at the door. Braden caught her around the waist and swung her away.

"Stop. We have to get out of here. You heard what he said about a gun. Let's go. I'm sorry about your da, but you can't stay here."

Amy looked up at Braden and met his sad eyes. She'd known he carried a weight, though he'd carefully avoided talking about anything personal. His sadness came from grief. She recognized it because it echoed everything she felt.

"You have lost someone, too," she whispered.

Braden's eyes darkened as if a cloud had gone over the sun and turned the blue sky gray. He held her gaze silently, then at last, as if it hurt to move his head, he nodded.

She had no one in the world who cared if she lived or died. Nowhere in the world to call home.

"Papa." Her knees buckled, the world swirled around, and her vision faded to black.

≈

Braden caught Amy as she collapsed, and swung her into his arms. He held her close, saw the utter whiteness of her skin. The frail woman weighed next to nothing, so he lifted her a bit higher in his arms.

"You're my strength, Braden."

His strength hadn't been enough for Maggie. Now, without any wish to provide it, he'd have to be the strength for Amy. He turned back toward the river. Ahead, he saw Wily disappear around a curve in the ever-narrowing water. The days were nearly split twelve hours of dark, twelve hours of light this time of year. It was just past noon, the sun high in the sky. They had miles to go, and darkness would catch them soon enough.

Alaska, the land of the midnight sun. What had he been thinking to come here?

Ian expected him. There'd been time to write, assuming a letter got out this far, but no time to get a response. Braden hadn't left immediately after Maggie died. He couldn't abandon his father that way, even though every day spent in the house where he and Maggie had lived with his parents and little sister was pure torture. Braden had stayed three months, finishing spring work; then he'd walked away before he could fail anyone else. Deep inside, he knew walking away added to his failures.

When he announced his plans to live in Alaska, his mother cried and scolded. Da turned quiet and spent a lot of time in the barn. His sister, Fiona, harangued him with her quick Irish tongue. Still, he'd left. Staying hurt too badly.

When he rounded the river bend, he saw Wily ahead, pulling his umiak as if it were a well-trained dog. The river flowed slightly deeper here. Braden couldn't see any rocks through the crystal clear water. He could ask Wily to let Amy ride, but he wouldn't. As much as he resented the burden she'd added to his life, her grief was too new. Only a monster would expect her to endure it alone.

Just for today, he'd be her strength.

❧

"Your brother's house is up that slope."

Braden's head came up and followed the direction indicated by Wily's gnarled finger.

He'd made it. They'd been walking for nearly twenty hours now, with only the most meager moments to rest. But they were here at last. Wily had taken him nearly to his brother's back door.

In the full moonlight, Braden made out a cabin barely outlined against the trees.

"I'll see to the load. You get the little one out of the night air." Wily had smeared some flat, strong smelling leaves on his skin and insisted Braden do the same and also use it to protect Amy. Though the swarm of bugs didn't bite, they buzzed around Braden until the air was thick with them.

Amy, her faint changing to a more natural slumber, had slept the afternoon and evening away in Braden's arms.

"Thanks. Come on up to the house for the night."

Wily shook his head. "Downstream's a sight faster'n up. I'll sleep at home tonight." Then the grizzled old man had given Amy a worried look. "Uh, mister, I'm right sorry I didn't warn Amaruq about her pa. I thought she knew. I'm never one to talk out of turn. But I'd a spared her that if'n I'd a known she 'spected to find her father to home."

With a shake of his head, Wily turned and began unloading the umiak.

Amaruq? What did that mean? A native word of affection for Amy, most likely. Braden turned toward Ian's house. He followed a path that climbed and twisted into the forest. Hoping Amy's extended unconsciousness came from simple exhaustion and shock and not something more serious, he reached Ian's door. "Ian, open up!"

A shout of joy sounded from inside the cabin. "Merry! He's here!"

The door flew open. "Braden, it's great to—" Ian, standing there in red flannel long johns, quit yelling. His expression faded from pure happiness to worry as he looked at Amy. Then he slung his arms around Braden awkwardly, trying not to squish Amy, but as if he couldn't contain his need to make contact.

"It's so great to see you. What happened? Who is she?"

Before Braden could speak, a pretty brunette in a hastily donned blue gingham housedress came dashing up from behind Ian. Ian stepped back just inches from Braden as if he couldn't bear to be farther away. A furrow cut through Ian's brow.

"You look done in, Braden. Let me take her." Ian reached for Amy, but Braden shook his head and angled away from Ian.

"Thanks, but I'm fine. I'll take her the rest of the way." Empty arms seemed like an extension of an empty life, and Braden couldn't face letting go right now. Bleakness washed over him.

" 'Tis a long walk from Skaguay." Ian stepped back a bit and laid a hand on Braden's shoulder.

Braden nodded. "I've left some supplies on the shore."

"This is Meredith." Ian tipped his head at his pretty, brown-haired wife. Ian's smile glowed with affection. Jealous pain slashed through Braden's heart.

Meredith nodded with a welcoming smile. "You must be exhausted. Is the woman hurt? Does she need medical care?"

Braden shook his head. "This is Amy Simons. She planned to return to her father's home. Peter Simons owns a cabin a few miles down river."

Ian nodded. "Knew him. He was an old trapper who's been here longer'n most anyone except the Eskimos. Never heard tell he had a daughter, though. Of course, he didn't talk much. Rumor had it he died last winter."

"Amy just found out."

"Let's get her inside. We can talk." Ian stopped and turned toward the river. "Say, is there coffee in those supplies?"

"We got one letter from you this year. Ma got so excited she sent everything you asked for and more. Let me lay Amy down. Then I'll see to it."

"You've got to be hungry." Ian nodded toward the house. "Let's get Amy to bed. Then you can eat while I holler for Tucker to help haul in the goods."

Braden knew of Meredith's twin, who had staked a claim nearby. "I didn't come here to make more work for you, Ian."

"If there's coffee in that pack you brought, I'll carry *you* down to the riverside, dancing all the way."

Braden scoffed. "That I'd like to see, little brother."

Grinning, Ian said, "I hardly qualify as your *little* brother anymore."

Braden noticed how broad Ian stretched across the shoulders these days. That kind of muscle came from long days swinging a pick for gold and an axe for wood. Braden wanted that kind of work. He wanted exhaustion that made him forget the torment of his memories.

Braden followed his brother into a tiny bedroom and lay Amy on the rumpled sheets. Ian and Meredith had obviously been long asleep when he arrived. Meredith pushed past him as he let his burden go with surprising reluctance.

Meredith busied herself fretting over Amy. He saw strength in Meredith's slim shoulders. She'd make a fine partner.

He couldn't stop his mind from turning to Maggie and all

her frailties and complaints about the rugged life. The guilt hit him with an edge as keen as an axe. Feeling as if he were betraying her memory, Braden decided that tomorrow he'd start earning his keep. He wouldn't be a burden to his brother. He wouldn't.

six

Amy's eyes flickered open. She stared at the ceiling overhead and wondered where she was. A noise made her turn her head, and she saw woodlands through an open window. The cool, crisp air and the sharp, sweet smell of cedar cleared her head. Alaska. Home.

Papa.

The memory hit her hard. A cry of pain nearly erupted from her throat. She choked it back, and it felt as if she swallowed jagged stones.

She'd never see her father again.

Fighting tears, she pushed the thick bearskin cover aside. The room felt sharply cold in the spring morning, but she'd been comfortable beneath the heavy fur. As she moved, her muscles protested.

Before she could sit up, the door opened, and a young woman entered.

"I thought I heard you moving in here." The pretty, dark-haired lady carried a tray. Amy could see a plate piled high with eggs, most likely duck eggs this time of year. Someone who knew the woods could feast in the spring. The plate had a slab of meat on it, too. Amy smelled mutton. If she'd been home, her father would have gone fishing early and brought in fresh salmon for breakfast.

Her eyes spilled over.

The woman set the tray down on a short table and dropped onto the bed beside Amy. "I'm Meredith, Braden's sister-in-law.

Braden told us you just found out your father died. I'm so sorry, Amy." The woman wrapped her arms around Amy's shoulders and pulled her close.

Braden had talked about his brother and his new wife. The future had been safe to discuss; it was the past he'd avoided. Amy couldn't resist the warm arms. She held on tight and cried her eyes out.

When the storm had spent itself, Meredith eased Amy away.

Amy saw tears on the kind woman's face.

"I'm so sorry about your father." Meredith drew a square of cloth from her apron pocket. She handed it to Amy, then dried her own eyes on her apron. "I know we can't begin to take the place of your father, but please stay with us. I was so thrilled to see Braden bring a woman yesterday, I nearly cried at the sight of you. I'm so lonely for a woman's company, I told Ian I was about to head out for Seattle to kidnap a woman off the street, bring her here, and force her to talk to me." Meredith smiled. "You've saved me a lot of trouble."

Amy burst out laughing. Somehow the laughter was almost as wrenching as the tears. "You mean I'm a prisoner?"

"Don't even think of trying to escape. I'm a desperate woman."

Amy smiled. "So, you just survived your first Alaskan winter, then?"

Meredith's eyes widened into perfect circles. "It's dark for six months!"

Amy felt the smile hold, which shocked her when her heart hurt so badly. She couldn't remember ever being this fond of someone on so short an acquaintance. "I lived in Alaska until the age of twelve when my mother died. I noticed the long winters."

"You'd better eat your breakfast. You're going to need plenty of strength to sit and listen to me talk for the next six weeks." Meredith reached for the tray and slid it in front of Amy. Arching her eyebrows, she said, "Make it six months."

"I don't need breakfast in bed. I'll come out to the kitchen." Amy tried to set the tray aside.

"No, that'll take too long. You just start eating. I'll tell you about my life. When you're done eating, it will be your turn. It all started when I came up here to live with my twin brother, Tucker."

Amy enjoyed every bite of the breakfast. She'd forgotten the special flavor of duck eggs. The bighorn sheep reminded her that her father had shot and smoked one every year but the tough, stringy, savory meat was a treat, not something to be eaten every day. They mainly ate salmon, halibut, seal, and even an occasional bit of whale when Amy's Tlingit relatives came past on their way north after a successful sea hunt.

They'd eaten the meat of whatever he trapped for fur, if possible. Mother made muskrat into a tasty stew combined with the greens and roots she'd coax out of the cold Alaskan dirt.

Amy would have had lapses into grief if Meredith hadn't chattered on while Amy ate, talking about her family and pointing out the window she'd had Ian add to the room so that they could get better air movement. Amy knew from Meredith's kind expression that the lady was deliberately putting herself out to be comforting.

When Amy finished her meal, Meredith said, "I've been heating water so you can have a warm bath."

Amy sat forward so eagerly she nearly fell out of bed. "Warm water?"

"Yes, and plenty of it. There's wood to burn and water to

heat if nothing else. Especially now that spring is here and we don't need to burn constantly just to keep the bitter cold at bay."

"Thank you. You shouldn't have. I could have bathed in the river." Amy'd done it many times and learned to think of the icy water as invigorating. Still, a warm bath was one of the things she'd liked best about Seattle.

Meredith shuddered. "Many's the time I've bathed in the river. You'll have to do it, too. But not this first time—not when you're so exhausted from the trip and drained from the awful news."

The mention of her father twisted Amy's wounded heart. "Is Braden here?" She saw the curious gleam in Meredith's eyes and wished she'd held her tongue.

"Yes, he's staying with us of course. He slept nearly as long and hard as you did. But he's already up and going strong. He's like his brother and mine when it comes to work. Our lives will be much easier with three men to do the heavy chores. It kept Tucker and Ian hopping to heat both cabins."

"You'll meet Tucker at dinner." Another gleam came into Meredith's eyes.

Amy could imagine what Meredith was thinking this time. The teachers at the mission had tried to persuade Amy to court. But she'd always planned to return to Alaska. No sense attaching herself to some man who might not want to come.

"I know you'll like my brother. We. . ."

Settling back a bit until Meredith wound down again, Amy enjoyed the talk of Meredith's family. A movement drew her attention, and she saw Braden standing in the open door, holding a steaming bucket in one hand and a large wooden tub in the other.

Amy reached quickly to tug on Meredith's sleeve. Meredith

looked at Amy, then turned to the door.

Rising from the bed, she said, "Bring it in, Braden. Don't let it cool.

Amy waited until she stood alone in her room, then quickly prepared for her bath. She longed to soak her aching muscles, but there was too much to do for her to linger. She'd already wasted a good part of the day in bed. She could see by the sunlight climbing the bedroom wall through the window that she'd slept half the morning away. She finished her tub bath in mere minutes even with taking the time to unbraid her hair and wash it with the bit of soap Meredith had left.

Amy combed and braided her hair while it was still wet. She pulled her other dress out of her satchel and slipped it on, then washed out her clothes and draped them on nails on the wall. Then she stepped out to the main room to see if she could be of use.

The first thing Amy noticed was a lovely window in the opposite wall. Someone had taken time and love to create it. A glass window was hard to come by in Alaska because glass was so fragile. But this window had been made with bottles of different colors. A cross had been fashioned from deep brown bottles in the center of it. Amy had already sensed Meredith had God in the center of her life, and this window just made it all the more certain from whom this family drew its strength.

The front door stood wide open, and Meredith worked outside, leaning over a table.

Amy wanted to go to Braden and thank him for getting her here yesterday. She couldn't remember anything after she left her father's house. Braden had stepped in, as he had the whole trip, and taken care of her. She felt shy to talk to him for some reason, so she took a step toward Meredith and froze.

For the first time, she noticed the crates Braden had brought up the river with him. They were piled high throughout the cabin. Amy's eyes widened at the things that draped out of the boxes and sat here and there on the floor.

Pure garbage.

A white and gold china figurine of a fine lady, her hair piled high on her head, holding out her long skirts as if to curtsy. Bolts of cloth—pretty but lightweight and impractical. A set of glass dishes. Only a few plates and cups survived intact.

A mantel clock, large and ornate. Amy shook her head. The clock ticked away on the roughly built kitchen table that took up half the room. But what did time matter in Alaska? Time was simple: dark and light, winter and not winter. Besides, the Raffertys didn't have a mantel. She remembered the Simonovich cabin did. The beautiful mantel in her father's cabin had been carved by her grandfather. The contents of its hidden drawer might prove her father hadn't sold the cabin.

She had to go back. She had to open that secret drawer. If her father had sold the cabin, the deed would be signed over to the new owner. If the deed still lay hidden in that drawer, then the man had taken the cabin and perhaps even killed her father.

A wave of grief stopped her from charging outside and heading straight for her father's house. She wasn't even sure how much farther they'd come upstream, although she had no doubt she'd find her way home without trouble. She needed to wait until she'd regained her strength, and she needed to repay the Raffertys for their kindness.

Amy walked outside in the spring warmth and sunlight, savoring the feel of a cool breeze against her damp hair. She noticed Braden splitting logs and approached Meredith. "Why is Braden doing that, Meredith?"

Meredith, standing over a cobbled-together table and

slicing sheep steaks, straightened. "Call me Merry, please. He's chopping wood." Meredith smiled. "Who knows why? Ian told him to pick it up off the ground, but Braden seems determined to do it the hard way."

Amy glanced at the tidy stone fireplace on the side of the cabin. "What he's splitting is too fresh. If he picks up windfall branches, they're already cured. The fresh wood smokes."

Meredith, her hands covered in blood from her carving, looked a little pale, but she smiled. "We told him all that. He just said he needed to work off some energy, and it'd be cured by winter. Which is true. Ian told me to leave him to it. I think it has something to do with Maggie. He must need to keep busy."

"Who is Maggie?"

Meredith's eyes widened. "I thought you'd traveled here together. He said he met you on the ship."

"We did."

"He never told you that his wife died three months ago, giving birth to their first child?"

Amy's grief, fresh and deep, swept over her. She remembered that moment when Braden had faced her at Papa's cabin. She'd known he mourned someone. Tears burned her eyes. "No, he never told me."

Meredith shook her head. "I'm sorry to have spoken of it. You're thinking of your father now; I can see."

There was no time to spare for tears. Amy dashed to wipe them away, then straightened her spine and turned to the day's chores. "Why are you having sheep again? It's tough, and they're heavy to cart home. The skins are nice, but I prefer bearskin or sealskin." Amy clamped her mouth shut, realizing she sounded rude. She'd always had trouble not speaking her mind.

Meredith calmly turned to a pail of water and washed her hands; then she took off her bloody apron and tossed it over a tree stump that stood next to her makeshift table. Without warning, she whirled around, launched herself the few feet separating her from Amy, and hugged her.

Amy staggered back. Her healing ribs protested, but she caught Meredith and hugged her back. "What is it?"

Amy looked over Meredith's shoulder and saw Braden pause in his chopping to look at them and arch an eyebrow. Amy shrugged.

Whispering, Meredith said, "I'm so sick of mutton I could die!" Her voice broke. Amy felt Meredith's shoulders shudder, and tears dripped onto her neck. Amy controlled the urge to smile.

Braden shook his head and disappeared into the woods, no doubt walking past perfectly cured wood lying at his feet to do things the hard way.

"The reason we're eating it right now is that Ian and Tucker love fresh meat. So do I as a rule. We need to refill the smokehouse before winter, but in the meantime, my menfolk want fresh steaks!"

"What about salmon? It's time for the salmon runs."

Meredith nodded. "Ian's been watching the river. He'll bring in a good supply of that, soon."

"I know a place a few miles downstream that's away from the river. I'm not sure how far we came yesterday, but that stream may be closer to you than it was to my home. I'll find it. My mother and I used to spear enough fish to last all winter with only a couple of days work."

Tears filled Meredith's eyes. "That sounds good. But for now, I've got to finish cutting the steaks off this beast, then cut the rest in strips so I can start smoking it." Her shoulders sagged, and she looked over her shoulder at the raw meat.

"I'll smoke the meat, Merry."

Meredith dashed her wrist across her eyes. "I'm just being silly today. I'm sorry. It seems I cry at the drop of a hat these days. I'll finish this. I'm almost ready to light a fire in the smokehouse. Go tell Braden to stop chopping and start picking up the wood that's lying thick on the ground." Meredith smiled, then turned back to her chore, fastening her apron firmly around her slender middle.

Amy turned to hunt up Braden, and for the first time she really saw the cabin.

Tiny.

Amy's face heated up as she realized the cabin had only one little room tacked on, and she'd taken it. The log cabin, little more than twelve-feet square before the extra room half that size was added, had barely enough floor space for three people to lie on the floor.

She'd ousted Meredith and Ian from their bedroom. Well, that couldn't happen again, not for one single night. But she couldn't share a room with Braden. What could she do? She headed around the cabin to tell Braden his long morning's work was a waste of time.

seven

"And then she has the nerve to tell me I'm wasting my time." Braden's irritation with the little woman wouldn't ease as he tromped through the trees. He'd have ignored her if she hadn't told him Meredith agreed.

Braden picked up sticks, Amy's voice taunting him. *Just pick wood up off the ground. It's a fraction of the work, and it's cured and ready to use.*

He filled his arms a dozen times, admitting the pile of wood grew far faster than when he'd split logs. Amy picked up sticks, too, although he'd deliberately gone in a different direction from her for fear of what he'd say in his irritated state.

He should have gone mining with Ian and Tucker, but he'd wanted to stay here and start earning his keep. He emptied his arms and turned to go into the woods again when Meredith came outside carrying a small bundle covered with a large gingham cloth. Braden recognized it as being among the things he'd brought from home. He still winced with embarrassment when he remembered the clock. He'd been in Alaska a day and already learned time didn't matter.

"Did you notice the cabin up the river, on past Tucker's?" Meredith asked.

"I saw a trail leading off that way, but I haven't followed it. I thought Ian wrote to us about a man who lived across the river from you, quite a character. Abrams, isn't it? Someone else lives around here?"

Meredith sighed. "If you can call it living. You're right about Mr. Abrams. He lives across the river. But Mr. Clemment lives on our side of the river, and I've been feeding him since the first chinook blew. Ian went to see how he'd come through the winter. Not everyone can endure six months of dark. He's not. . .thinking clearly."

"Not thinking clearly?" Braden narrowed his eyes at his sweet new sister. "What does that mean?"

Meredith shrugged and handed Braden what turned out to be a plate, still warm. "Just leave this at Mr. Clemment's cabin and bring back the dishes from yesterday. I don't have any to spare. And Braden?"

"Yes?"

"Uh, if Mr. Clemment should happen to be on his roof when you get there. . ." Meredith lapsed into silence.

"He's repairing the roof?"

"No, he. . .well. . .sometimes he thinks he needs to. . ." Another extended silence. "He's usually down by now."

"Meredith. . ." Braden drew her name out slowly and shifted his weight impatiently.

"He's harmless." Meredith scuffed one foot on the still-frozen ground and clasped her hands behind her back as if afraid Braden would hand the dish back. "In fairness, it helps Tucker get up in the morning."

Braden's eyes fell closed. "Tell me what's going on."

Ian came up the sloping hill, spotted the cloth, and said, "Don't tell Rooster Clemment he's not a chicken. He gets mad."

"Rooster?" Braden looked at the seemingly sane pair.

"He climbs the roof every morning and crows, right at dawn—except in the winter. We suspect he just stayed up there waiting, hoping the sun would rise."

"He stayed on his roof all winter? An Alaskan winter?" Braden felt his eyebrows arch nearly to his hairline.

Ian looked at Meredith. "Probably not. He's alive, after

all. We were shut in pretty tight ourselves, so we really didn't check. We just went to see him this spring and found him up there." He shrugged. "When we began having a few minutes of daylight, Rooster'd crow it up, then crow it down. Now I think he's afraid to come down. He doesn't make much sense most of the time. But based on a couple of things he said, I believe he thinks the sun will go down if he isn't up there."

Braden shook his head in disbelief.

Ian grinned at him. "Anyway, say hello whether he's on the roof or not. He gets mad if you ignore him. Then go on inside, get the old plates and leave the new. He's harmless."

"If he's harmless, why do I have to worry about making him mad?"

Ian appeared to be thinking that over. "Maybe I should take the food."

Braden rolled his eyes, then set off with the plate, still warm to the touch.

Ian called after him, "If he laid any eggs, go ahead and bring 'em home!"

"Ian," Meredith chided, "be nice."

Braden glanced back to see her cuff Ian on the arm. Ian started laughing, grabbed Meredith around the waist, and swung her in a circle while she giggled.

The stab of jealousy shamed him, and Braden turned away. He didn't begrudge Ian his marriage to such a sweet lady as Meredith. But it reminded him that he'd never touch his Maggie again. Seeing Ian's happiness hurt.

Braden passed Tucker's neat little cabin in a tiny clearing. It was one room built just for a gold miner who spent all his life outdoors, panning in an icy stream or slamming his pickax into a hillside. Tucker didn't spend any time there except for sleeping. He even ate all his meals with the Raffertys, which Ian said was fair because Tucker helped hunt the food and cooking for three was as easy as cooking for two.

Ian and Tucker admitted at breakfast that they hadn't made a big strike. They found enough color to support themselves but not enough to draw their own herd of stampeders. Both men thought it was a good tradeoff.

He walked on. A few steps farther, Amy came out of the woods with an armload of branches. As he reached her side, he saw a barely visible game trail climb up the sheer, heavily wooded land that hugged the narrow path. How had she found that tiny trail so quickly? Her hair dangled loose from her braid, and dirt smudged her face here and there. She had a bag slung over her shoulder, the same one she'd carried all the way from Seattle. The bag bulged, and what looked like a slab of bark stuck out the top. Twigs and leaves had snagged her dress and tangled in her hair as if she'd fought her way through a bramble. But she didn't complain or fuss at her appearance. His Maggie had always been so tidy.

"You should be resting." Braden clamped his mouth shut before he could say anything else. Whether Amy wore herself out wasn't his concern.

Amy smiled. "I intend to help wherever I can. I have no wish to be a burden to Ian and Merry. What are you doing?" She nodded at the dish in his hands.

"Near as I can tell, I'm feedin' the chickens."

A smile quirked her lips. "There are not any chickens in Alaska." She dropped her load of sticks in a neat pile alongside the trail and dusted off her hands. Coming close, she peeked under the cloth. "And if there were, we would not give them mutton for breakfast."

"Want to come along? I might need someone watching my back trail." Braden hadn't meant to invite her along. The words just came out.

"In case you are attacked by a flock of the chicken's friends?"

Amy turned and walked beside him on the trail. Braden realized they'd become friends on the trip here. They'd talked a lot on that long, boring journey but not said much about their pasts. Memories of Maggie still rubbed too raw. But they'd talked plenty about their ideas for the future in Alaska. Both of them trying to stay out of the stampeders' way. Neither of them held much interest in gold—the only interest for everyone else.

Hitching her bag higher on her shoulder, Amy stretched out her stride to match his, even though her legs were much shorter. "Braden, I want to go back to my father's cabin. I need to be sure that man has a legal claim. I can do that if I can get inside. Father had the deed hidden, but I know where it is."

"I'm real sorry about your da, Amy. But what good would it do to go back? You can't live there alone."

The trail disappeared ahead, around a curve of rock. Braden saw the stubborn set of Amy's jaw and knew she'd commence to nagging any second. When the cabin appeared right around the bend, he breathed a sigh of relief and changed the subject. "I can't believe how close the cabins are to each other."

"No use for forty acres here." Amy seemed to drink in the beauty around her, looking into the heavily wooded land that barely made room for this narrow path. A stream chuckled through the little clearing, and sunlight cut through the towering pines to bathe the gap in sunlight.

Braden had to admit the scenery looked breathtaking. "True enough. No one's planting a corn crop."

"But about my father. I think. . . ." Amy fell silent.

As the cabin came fully into view, Braden saw a man standing on the roof on one leg, his hands tucked into his armpits. The man stared up at the beams of sunlight as if he were soaking himself in them. Braden—now understanding Ian's amusement—exchanged a look with Amy. Her brow furrowed. Her dark eyes gleamed with compassion.

"Good morning, Mr. Clemment." Braden tried to remember all the ways Ian had said you could make Rooster mad. "I'm Ian Rafferty's brother. I've brought you some dinner."

The man lowered his curled leg to the roof and jammed his hands on his hips. *Uh oh, that looks like mad.* Then the man, with a head of brown hair and a full beard sticking in all directions like a dark sunburst around his face, stuck his arms back where they'd been. He flapped his elbows as if he planned on taking off, looked at the sky, and crowed at the top of his lungs.

"You take the food in, Braden. Let me talk to Mr. Clemment for a while."

"I'd better stay out here instead. You maybe shouldn't be alone with him. There's no telling what he might get up to."

"He looks harmless to me, except maybe to himself." Amy began walking toward the house.

Harmless. Probably true. Ian had said so. Glancing up at the man, he whispered to Amy. "Yell if you need me."

Amy threw him a confused look as if unable to imagine ever possibly needing him.

Braden went into the tiny cabin to set the food on the table. There wasn't one. The cabin was packed to the rafters with wood, bark, furs, and leaves. Braden had walked into a nest.

A trail of trampled down sticks led to the middle of the room. In the center of the chaos, as if Clemment *had* laid an egg, were a few plates like the one Braden carried—no doubt Meredith's. Braden set the food down, picked up the used plates—still dirty, but Braden didn't expect a chicken to wash dishes—and picked his way outside.

When he stepped outside, Amy had vanished. "Amy, where'd

you go?" Braden turned in a circle, looking for her. His heart sped up. A cold sweat broke out on his forehead. Before he could holler again or step back far enough to see Rooster, Wily and another man approached the cabin by the trail Braden and Amy had used. Then Braden heard voices. Turning, he saw Amy sitting on the roof, chatting with Rooster Clemment. Rooster had settled down on the peak of the roof beside her, his knees drawn up to his chest, and his arms clamped around them.

The man with Wily approached Braden. "If you're Ian Rafferty, thank you for contacting me and telling me about my brother. I'm here to take him home."

"I'm Braden Rafferty. Ian's my brother."

"Well whoever you are, thank you. We had no idea where Wendell had gone." The man reached a hand out to Braden, who balanced the plates in one hand and shook with the other.

"You've restored my brother to me. God bless you." The man pulled a piece of paper from his pocket. He scribbled on it, lay it face down on the gingham cloth, and turned to the man on the roof.

"Wendell, come down!"

Rooster, busy visiting with Amy, turned at the sound. From the ground, Braden could see the man's eyes widen with recognition. "Carlton?"

Rooster slid down the roof, dismounting as gracefully as if he really could fly, and flung himself at the man. Braden could smell Rooster from twenty feet away.

The newcomer didn't so much as flinch as he pulled Rooster into his arms. "Father and Mother and I want you to come home. We miss you so much. Please say you'll come with me."

Rooster pulled free of his brother's arms and looked back at his cabin.

Amy dropped off the roof and came to rest her hand on Rooster's arm. "The sun shines for long hours all winter back home. You need to go, Wendell."

Wendell looked at the sky, then back at the roof as if he were worried about abandoning his vigil.

"It will be fine, Wendell." Amy patted his shoulder. "I will see to your work here. Your family needs you. Think of the sunlight and warmth. There are no long days of darkness where your brother is going."

"You remember Texas, don't you? Even in winter, we have warm days and lots of sun," Carlton added.

Rooster nodded but seemed hesitant. A man who thought he crowed the sun up wouldn't want to leave his post. Braden admired Rooster's dedication.

Between Amy and Carlton, Rooster allowed himself to be talked into leaving, walking away from the cabin with nothing. What would he pack anyway? Sticks?

Braden stood quietly nearby with Wily.

Carlton and Rooster—one dressed for civilization in a suit adorned with Wily's walrus intestine boots, the other dressed in rags—their arms slung around each other, headed down the trail.

Wily muttered, "Alaska ain't for everybody."

Braden wasn't sure which man Wily was talking about. "How'd you get back up here so fast? You've barely had time to walk home."

Wily shrugged. "I kin catch a current home and ride most of the way. Mr. Clemment stood there a'waitin' for me when I arrived, half crazed with worry 'bout Rooster. He convinced me to turn around and hightail it back."

Braden looked at the gaunt man. His weathered skin barely showed through his beard. "You must be exhausted."

Wily twisted his beard into a long, gray rope. "I been tired a'fore. I reckon I'll be tired agin." He trudged down the trail after the Clemments.

As the men disappeared from sight, Amy came up beside Braden. "I am glad his brother came. He needed to go home."

Which reminded Braden that Amy needed to go home. Not Ian's home but civilization home—Seattle. "While you were talking Rooster down off the roof, Carlton said Ian wrote to him and told him Wendell wasn't well. He thanked me. I didn't do anything."

"I am sure they did not want to take the time to hunt up Ian and thank him. What is that paper he gave you?"

Braden looked at the folded paper on top of the crumpled gingham. Shifting the plates, he unfolded the paper.

"A deed to Rooster's claim." Braden looked after the men and took a step after them. "He wrote Braden Rafferty on it. He meant it for Ian not me."

Amy caught his arm. "Do not worry about it. If you want Ian to have it, just sign it over."

Braden nodded. "Yep, that's okay then. Ian can have it."

❧

Ian didn't want it.

"So, Rooster's brother came and got him?" Ian studied the handwritten note Carlton Clemment had scribbled Braden's name on.

Meredith straightened from the table, where she snipped at green wool for Ian's shirt. She folded the cloth with sharp, tidy snaps. "That's good. He needed to go home."

"How'd you get up on that roof so fast?" Braden asked Amy, who set the little bag she'd kept at her side all the way from Seattle in the corner of the kitchen.

"Flew up just like Rooster does?" Ian offered the deed back to Braden.

Amy smiled, shook her head, and said nothing.

"I'm not taking it." Braden tucked his hands in his pockets. "You and Merry've been caring for him. You'll be the ones takin' his claim, and that's that."

Amy crouched on the floor by the wall, her bag beside her. Braden watched her digging around in what looked like twigs and crushed leaves. What had she gathered that for? Kindling?

"Stubborn big brother." Ian narrowed his eyes, then shoved the paper into the breast pocket of Braden's brown broadcloth shirt. "I don't need another claim. This isn't like Oregon where we want to add to our acreage to grow more crops. I'm getting a living out of the rock I'm hacking at now. A few ounces of gold a month trickle out of there. We don't need much cash money. And I'm as busy as I want to be."

"But what if there's a big gold strike on Rooster's land? It should be yours."

Ian looked at Meredith. "He's right. I could be handin' away a fortune."

Meredith's eyes twinkled. "Why do I doubt that?"

Ian laughed, and Meredith joined in. "Keep the claim, Braden. The house is the real gold mine."

Braden thought about the mess inside Rooster's house. *Why do I doubt that?*

"We're too crowded here." Meredith tucked the fabric into one of the wooden boxes Braden had brought that nearly filled the little cabin. "And if God wants Ian to strike it rich, he will. He won't have to go around grabbing up every claim that comes his way."

Ian nodded. "I'd rather hunt than dig any day. We can't eat gold."

Amy smiled. "That sounds very Alaskan of you."

Tucker came in carrying a platter of raw steaks. Braden noticed Meredith turn from her brother and move to the open window. She stood casually looking out and breathing slowly. But her stance struck Braden as deliberate.

Braden pulled the deed out. "I can live in the house without owning it."

Tucker gave his sister a close look that made Braden wonder if the two of them were up to something. "I saw Wily going downriver with Rooster and another man. What's going on?"

"Rooster's brother came to get him." Braden quickly told Tucker what had happened that morning.

"Wasn't Wily just here last night?" Tucker looked away from his sister, then began to skewer the steaks with a pointed metal spit and hang them over the gently crackling flames in the fireplace.

"He told me he'd sleep in Skaguay," Braden remembered. "Downstream's faster than up, and he expected to get home before it got too late."

Ian nodded. "True enough. Rooster's brother must have pushed him hard."

Amy rose from digging around in her bag, and Braden noticed her favoring her ribs. His thoughts went back to Rooster's house. "Why'd you go up on the roof anyway? You could have fallen off and gotten yourself killed."

Amy turned and sank into one of Ian's roughhewn chairs. "I've seen people driven half mad by the long winter before. I hoped I could talk some sense into him—talk him into going back down south. He let me pray with him. Then just when we were praying, his brother came as if God Himself had sent help."

Tucker added sticks to the fire.

"Here's how it's gonna be, big brother." Ian laughed and slapped Braden on the shoulder hard enough that Braden nearly staggered. "You're taking the claim."

Braden felt his jaw tighten. "I might be robbing my own

brother of a fortune. I won't do it."

"Braden." Ian shook his head, grinning. "There's no great wealth to be chiseled out'a those rocks."

Braden didn't want to take the chance of striking it rich and alienating his brother forever. "I'll take the claim, but anything I find, we share."

Ian shrugged. "Sounds fair enough if you'll agree to the same thing on my claim. I don't want you digging on Rooster's claim anyway. I want you digging on mine."

"I'm not taking half your gold!"

Tucker straightened. "We always work together without much mind to which claim we're on. It's safer to stay together, and the isolation of working a claim gets to a man after a while."

"Like it did Rooster." Ian's gaze hardened. "So, I'll take your deal of sharing, Braden. A three-way split between you, me, and Tucker. And offer you the same deal back on my own claim."

"I'll take it." Braden couldn't imagine what he'd need gold for. But if he got any, he'd spend it on his brother and Meredith somehow or send it home to Da and Ma. "I need a house, and you need the space."

"Merry and I will do what straightening we can to your new house today," Amy said quietly. "I looked inside a window as I climbed up. It needs. . .quite a bit of work.

An understatement if Braden had ever heard one. He remembered Rooster's man-sized chicken coop. Braden wondered if he'd be the one on the roof next.

eight

"Have you been inside Rooster's cabin, Merry?" Amy and Meredith started down the path toward Braden's new cabin as soon as they'd cleaned up after lunch. Amy thought of the work ahead of them to turn a nest into a home.

The men were long gone exploring Rooster's claim.

"Oh my, yes. The contents of Rooster's house will make a year's worth of kindling. All we have to do is carry it outside."

"That's all, huh?" Amy and Meredith exchanged a dry look; then Merry started laughing. The urge to laugh surprised Amy. She'd always been very reserved with people, and she'd spent little time around women her age. There were some in the school, of course, but Amy went home only to the McGraws, who were wonderful to her but were more given to quiet smiles than to giggles.

The two of them set to work. Amy ignored her aching ribs. The pain was no longer sharp and frightening. Amy noticed that Meredith had turned pale and worked more slowly as the hours passed.

"Why don't you go back to the cabin and start supper? I can finish here."

The pale color of Meredith's cheeks took on a faintly greenish tinge, and her shoulders slumped. "There'll be mutton again tonight." She said the words like she was reading a death notice, then walked away.

Exhausted by the time the light faded from the sky, Amy swept the cabin free of the last bits of twigs and leaves, then hurried back to help Meredith. Amy's strength waned far too quickly. To make the meal more interesting, she gathered a few greens on her way. Noting a berry bush, Amy planned the dessert she would make when they were ripe.

She spotted a moss her mother had brewed into a tea that helped reduce fever and another useful in a poultice to prevent wounds from turning septic. She needed to lay in a supply of medicines, so she made a note of the location.

She stepped in the cabin just as Meredith set the steaks on to cook in a large iron kettle full of water. Meredith straightened from hanging the kettle and staggered backward.

Amy rushed forward and caught Meredith before she fell.

"Are you all right?" Amy turned Meredith to face her. Meredith's cheeks were ashen, and her eyes weren't focused.

"A–Amy?" Meredith groped for Amy's arm as if she couldn't see where to hang on.

"Sit down." Amy urged Meredith to the table, settling her on a chair.

Meredith folded her arms on the table and laid her head down. "I must have straightened up too suddenly."

"Are you feeling ill?" Amy ran a hand over Meredith's disheveled hair. Meredith's forehead glowed with sweat.

"No, don't worry about me. I'm fine." Meredith lifted her head, then looked toward the fireplace, clamped her mouth shut tight, and laid her head down again.

"Is the smell of the steak making you dizzy?" Amy couldn't imagine why that would be. Influenza had gone through the school in Seattle, but that kind of illness was rare in remote areas of Alaska. Other people had to bring the disease. If Amy had gotten sick on the boat and brought some sickness with her, that would make sense. But neither Amy nor Braden had experienced so much as a sniffle.

Meredith, her voice muffled by her arms and the table, said, "I think I need some fresh air."

Amy watched as Meredith raised her head and shoved herself to her feet. Amy didn't trust her not to fall again, so she took a firm grip on Meredith's arm and steadied her until they got outside.

The stump Braden had used to chop kindling stood only a few feet from the house. Amy helped Meredith reach it, then eased her down.

"I think I know what's wrong." Meredith lifted her head and managed a true smile, even though her skin carried the chalky white of a long blizzard.

"What?"

"It's better outside. I hadn't realized how much the smell of cooking meat bothered me."

"What is better? What is wrong?" Amy sorted through the illnesses her mother had taught her and the treatments. Did Meredith have a wound that had festered? Had she fallen and sustained some internal injury? Amy crouched down in front of Meredith to quiz her.

A secret smile on Meredith's lips stopped Amy's questions. A blush crept up Meredith's cheeks, erasing the frightening pallor as Meredith's hand slid to her stomach.

"I think I'm carrying Ian's child." A soft laugh escaped Meredith's lips, and she quickly moved one hand to catch the sound.

Amy dropped the rest of the way to the ground. "Really?" A smile spread across her face as she looked at Meredith's joyful expression.

"I've been wondering for a couple of weeks, but I wasn't sure. That must be it, don't you think?"

Amy knew something about babies and how they were born because her mother had occasionally been called in to do some doctoring for her people. Amy asked questions about Meredith's condition, and they decided together a baby was definitely on the way.

"Have you told Ian yet?" Amy clutched Meredith's hands, excited about the new baby.

The smiled faded from Meredith's face, and her pallor returned. "I'm afraid to even suggest it."

Amy got on her knees and leaned close to her friend. "But why?"

Meredith's lips curled down, and her eyes filmed over with tears. "Ian worries, and now that he's heard about Maggie's death. . ." Meredith shuddered. "Braden, Ian, and Maggie practically grew up together. I'm afraid to tell Ian I'm expecting. I know it will frighten him. He's already overprotective of me. This will make it worse."

"You are going to have to tell him, Merry. This is not the kind of thing a woman can hide for long."

"Oh, I know. I'll tell him soon. But now that I know I may have trouble cooking, he'll worry all the more. He's already so busy with the mine that he comes home exhausted every night. Now he'll think he needs to cook and do any lifting around the house. He'll take even more on himself. I understand that this stomach upset and the dizziness don't last. If I could just wait to tell him until I'm feeling stronger, I think he'd handle it better."

Amy nodded. "And Braden is going to be even worse than Ian."

Meredith took Amy's hand. "He seems so sad, and he has yet to even speak Maggie's name except when Ian asked him a direct question. Has he talked to you about her?"

"No, the first I knew his wife and child had died was when you told me about it this morning."

Meredith straightened and looked over her shoulder toward the woods. "Tucker will take his cue from Ian and Braden. I'll be lucky if the three of them don't order me to bed for the whole time. And I wouldn't mind them being so protective if it didn't land a burden on all of them."

Amy nodded. "Then here is what we will do. We will wait as long as possible to tell the men. In the meantime, I will help you with the things that upset your stomach like the cooking. We will get you outside in the fresh air every chance. Since I have newly arrived, maybe they will not realize you are doing a bit less, and I am doing more."

"But you're still exhausted from your trip."

"So, we will work together. Surely the two of us together, even in the shape we are in, equal one fully functioning woman."

Meredith's eyes got wide, then she erupted into laughter. The two of them hugged.

"Congratulations." Amy pulled away to arm's length. "This baby is going to be such a precious blessing to this home."

Meredith's eyes filled with tears of joy. "I can't wait." She hugged her stomach again.

Amy hopped to her feet. Despite her long day and lingering injuries, she felt renewed strength. "I am going in to finish the dinner. You rest a bit. If you are able, you can stack the branches Braden and I brought in today. I think the fresh air is all you need. When the meat is done cooking and the room airs out, I will call you in. Can you eat? Sometimes new mothers are nauseated."

Meredith shrugged. "I've had a good appetite so far. I think it's just the smell of it cooking that got to me. I've had several episodes like the one tonight, but no one caught me with my head on the table." Meredith stood and threw her arms around Amy. "Thank God for you, Amy." Meredith burst into tears.

Amy shook her head and patted Meredith on the shoulder until the tears eased. "I remember my mother saying crying at odd times was a symptom of a baby on the way."

Meredith dried her eyes on her apron. "Well, I've definitely got that."

"Sit back down for a while. Make sure your head is clear before you start bending and stacking the branches. And do not let me catch you lifting any heavy ones or I am telling Ian about the baby tonight."

Meredith nodded, then sat and folded her hands in her lap like a prim and proper school girl. "I'll behave, Mama. I promise."

Meredith dissolved into laughter, and Amy joined in.

Amy finally went to the house and set about preparing dinner for the Rafferty clan.

※

Swirling the pan, letting the crystal clear water overflow the edges, and watching for bits of gold, Braden hadn't seen a fleck of gold yet. He wished he'd catch gold fever because, unless he did, panning for gold was never going to be any fun. He didn't see much sign of the gold madness resting on Ian or Tucker, either. The only time they got interested as they worked about twenty feet apart on the icy murmuring stream was when they talked about hunting.

"I saw polar bear tracks a stone's throw from my house." Tucker worked the rocker with the steady swish of water against a sieve. Occasionally, he straightened and flicked at the bottom of his pan with a negligent finger, then tossed the contents away.

"Are you sure it wasn't a grizzly?" Ian sat on a rock, swishing away, staring into the pan. "I've never heard of a polar bear this far south."

The two men seemed to prefer working close enough to talk, showing none of the normal miner's ferocious knowledge of his property line. Braden wasn't even sure where the boundary of his claim lay. Of course, only the three of them were mining in the area, so who'd argue about property lines?

"There were tufts of pure white fur. The old boy must be shedding his winter coat because the fur scraped off as if he were snowing."

Ian looked at Tucker. "It'll be hungry and cranky. We'd better keep Merry close to the cabin."

"Amy, too." Braden tossed the slushy sediment back into the water. He saw a silver fish flash past in the fast-moving stream. He thought their time could be better spent fishing than mining.

"So, have you spoken for the little woman?" Tucker asked.

Braden straightened and looked at Ian's brother-in-law. "Of course not. I didn't come up here hunting for a woman."

"Hmmm. . ." Tucker kept rocking.

"What's that supposed to mean?" Braden couldn't hide his irritation. He wrestled his temper under control.

"Doesn't mean a thing." The quiet scratch of rock against metal almost covered Tucker's mild comment.

"Her father just died. She's not interested in any man right now."

"She tell you that?" Tucker, bent at the waist, working his rocker, turned his back to Braden.

Braden's eyes narrowed on Tucker. "Are you saying you're interested in Amy?"

"I'm not saying a thing. Asked a simple question is all. Just makin' conversation."

Braden frowned at Tucker's back. Then he glanced at Ian and saw Ian swirling his pan and watching Braden when he should be looking for gold dust.

Braden decided to change the subject. "So, you've actually found some gold here?"

Tucker laughed.

Ian tossed the contents of his pan away and grinned at

Braden. "We get some color out of here once in a while."

Tucker stood and tugged his suspenders. "I keep hoping I'll catch gold fever, but so far, this is just plain boring."

Ian grunted in agreement, then shrugged. "It pays the bills."

"What bills? I thought you lived off the land."

"Good thing, because gold wouldn't pay any. It's almost supper time." Ian packed his scanty supplies and gathered up his rifle. Braden and Tucker followed suit. "Let's go down the trail in the direction you saw the bear, Tucker. Seein' his tracks'd tell us what we're up against."

Companionably, the three of them began the hike through the heavy woods.

nine

For the next two weeks, Amy did the lion's share of the work, and Meredith got the credit.

Amy neatly rolled the pallet she slept on in the main room as Meredith talked to her through the window. "I feel like a fraud sitting out here day after day."

"You are working." Amy talked to Meredith through the cabin window as she set the salmon steaks on to roast in the covered skillet. "You have almost finished that shirt for Braden."

The day before, Amy had hiked to the spawning beds and speared enough salmon to last a month. She'd cleaned them at the stream to keep from luring hungry grizzlies to the cabin, then dragged them home with a travois she rigged out of cedar branches. Hanging them high in a tree a good distance from the house so a bear wouldn't get to them, she planned to spend the morning building a separate smokehouse for the salmon to separate the fishy smell from the bighorn sheep and other meat, then go fishing again in the afternoon. The salmon would run for two weeks. By the time they were done, she'd have enough to last the winter.

She'd seen bear sign between the cabin and the stream and was tempted to go hunting. The fur and lard would come in handy, and she loved bear meat. But it would be wiser to wait until the end of summer for that, when the bear's fur grew thick and its belly fat.

"Ian loved his shirt, didn't he?" Meredith got a faraway look in her eyes. Amy remembered Ian's delighted thank-you to

74

his wife when she showed him what she'd sewn. The affection between the two of them had awakened a longing in Amy, but for what she didn't know.

Ian had worn it for the very simple church service the Raffertys held each Sunday morning. Then, because the Raffertys kept the Sabbath and did no hunting or mining on Sunday, he'd worn it the rest of the day.

Braden had attended the service, but he remained solemn and offered nothing when Ian read the Scripture. Amy was nearly brought to silence when Ian read the verse that she'd so studiously ignored when she'd headed north.

Ian read from Isaiah the same verse Parson McGraw had read her when she lay mending in Seattle: *"But they that wait upon the Lord shall renew their strength; they shall mount up with wings as eagles; they shall run, and not be weary; and they shall walk, and not faint."*

Wait.

How clearly she'd heard God's urging. But what purpose did waiting serve? Her father was dead, and she needed to find out why and make sure justice was done. She turned her thoughts from that part of the morning's message and joined in with the group's discussion of God's blessing. She heard an eagle cry overhead, and her heart pounded more quickly as the encouraging words from Isaiah settled in her soul. Yes, those words called her to wait. But they also promised strength to soar, to run, to walk and not faint. A request from God and a promise in return for obedience.

Meredith needed strength. She needed to not be weary. With a sigh of relief, Amy claimed this verse for Meredith. It was good Amy had come to help out the family so Meredith could rest.

After their day of rest, Meredith chose a length of fabric to make another shirt, this one for Tucker.

Enjoying the feel of a piece of smooth, lightweight calico, Amy said, "I can't believe Mrs. Rafferty sent all those bolts of cloth." It served no purpose to make a dress of the calico. It wouldn't protect against mosquitoes in the summer, and it was too thin to keep a body warm in the winter.

"We could take it to Skaguay and sell it for a fortune." Amy shook her head at the waste.

"Well, we're not. We're keeping it all to ourselves. We'll be the best-dressed people in Alaska. And what doesn't work for clothing, we'll use for curtains and tablecloths." Meredith threaded a needle and knotted one end. She dug her needle into the soft flannel.

Amy saw Meredith finger the red plaid and envied her working with the bright, smooth cloth. Then the smell of the salmon teased her nose—a delicious smell she'd missed—and she decided she had the better of the two jobs.

Once the juniper berries were on to simmer, sprinkled with a bit of the precious sugar Mrs. Rafferty had sent, Amy headed outside and went to work, piling the stones for her smokehouse.

Wanting to build it well away from the cabin so the smoke wouldn't torment Meredith, Amy chose a spot near a tumbled pile of stones at the base of the mountain. The Rafferty's sturdy little log smokehouse stood close to their cabin, nearly depleted of stores after the long winter. Ian's recent luck hunting bighorn sheep had kept them fed, but Amy wanted a change of diet for Meredith. Starting with heavy flat stones for the foundation, she rolled them into a circle, wanting it big enough to get the dozens of salmon steaks all cooking at once.

She worked the morning away, carefully selecting stones that went well together. The tighter she made it, the faster the salmon would cook. Every foot, Amy left good-sized holes in the chimney, and by the holes, she rigged drying racks of fresh saplings.

The work reminded her of her childhood. Her mother had smoked salmon just this way. The pangs of loneliness for her papa still hit her hard at times, but she knew her papa's faith. Picturing him in heaven—surrounded by white-capped mountains and soaring eagles, sparkling, rushing streams. and heavily furred animals that now were his to caress without needing their fur for warmth—made her grief bearable. Then she thought of the man who lived in her father's house, and her anger burned. She needed to go back and find out if the sale was real. If not, that man might have. . .

Amy veered her thoughts away from the awful man and her father's fate. She couldn't go now. She had to care for Meredith. The need to gain justice for her father festered like a sliver embedded under her skin, but it would have to wait.

Sweating from exertion, Amy felt better than since before her accident. Using smaller and smaller stones, she narrowed the smokehouse, five feet across at its circular base, into a chimney. The stones were still heavy, nearly the size of a man's head, but her ribs didn't protest when she lifted them. She felt healthy and happy and at home. Just as the structure reached waist level, the trees rustled behind her.

With a start, she turned.

"What are you doing?" Braden dashed across the opening around Amy's smokehouse. He grabbed the rock she held as if it were preparing to drop on her head.

"I am drying salmon. Is it midday?" Amy wondered if she'd lost track of time. "I am sorry if your meal is late." She glanced at the sun, not quite overhead. If she hurried, she had time to finish the chimney, lay out the fish, and start a smoldering fire.

Dusting her hands, she pointed at the smokehouse. "Just rest the flat side right there."

Amy noticed his stunned expression as Braden laid the stone into place on the half-built wall. She turned and selected another rock.

"You did all this?" Braden shifted the piece of granite he'd taken from Amy.

Impressed with his feel for fitting the stone in place, Amy said, "Of course. We have to preserve the fish for winter."

"What fish?"

Amy reached for one of the cedar branches she'd laid over the salmon and flipped it aside. "These fish."

Braden's mouth gaped at the dozens of filets. "Where did you get all this?"

Amy tilted her head at the silly question. "Uh, the river? You know fish come out of the water, right?"

Braden pivoted to face her, his eyes narrow.

She grinned.

A spark of humor relaxed his features. "Yes, I know where fish come from."

"I went fishing yesterday afternoon. I left after you'd gone back to the gold mine and got home ahead of you. I forgot to mention it. The salmon are running. Meredith says Ian gets them out of the river, but I knew of a little stream nearby that angles off the Skaguay River." Amy arched her brows. "The one we came up to get here."

"I remember the Skaguay River." Braden crossed his arms. "I walked in ice water for half a day. I couldn't forget that river if I tried."

"Good." Mindful of the time, Amy grabbed a rock and set it on the narrowing smokehouse.

Braden took it from her. "Tell me where to set it."

"If you want to help, then get your own rock. I am not going to stand here and point while you do the work."

Braden set the rock in place, then stopped to stare at her as if he'd never seen a woman before. "You're going to help me?"

"Braden! I am not going to *help* you. I am going to do it myself. Maybe, if I am really lucky, you are going to help me. I have already finished with the hard part. We are to the little rocks now." She bent for another rock.

Braden grabbed it.

She held on, glared, and asked, "Do you not have some gold to mine?" She had a brief tug-of-war with Braden, her callused fingers slipping on the rough piece of rubble.

Then, as if the sun came out from under a cloud, a smile broke out across his face. It reached his eyes in a way she'd never seen before. "You'd throw me out and do it yourself?"

Amy jerked the rock free of Braden's hands. "I mean this in the nicest way possible, Braden, but get your own rock, or go away."

A gurgling sound startled Amy into looking at the pesky man. Braden was laughing. His voice tripped over the sound coming out of his throat as if he didn't remember quite how to laugh.

The laughter sang like sweet music in Amy's ears after seeing the weight of sadness Braden carried like a load of stones. The joy of the moment made her laugh, too. He released the rock when he laughed, and Amy set it in place. Then side-by-side they enjoyed the day and their silly argument and each other.

Ragged corners of Amy's heart, tattered from her father's death, knit together as she laughed with Braden. When the laughter faded, she remembered anew how this beautiful land had been like God's own cathedral when she was growing up, as if Alaska sat on the top of the world closer to heaven. Amy felt more at peace than she had since she'd left her northern home six years ago. Braden's laughter had brought her closer to God.

With a silent prayer of thanks and a quick flutter of her hand at Braden, Amy shook her head. "Enough nonsense. I am in a hurry. I have got to get dinner on." She grabbed another rock.

Braden hesitated for a second as if he seriously considered taking this stone from her, too. She angled her back to him to protect the rock.

Braden bent down and selected his own stone. "There's no hurry. Merry does all the cooking."

Amy froze with the rock resting on her smokehouse wall. In the closeness of the moment, she'd forgotten they'd been hiding the news of the baby from the men. Knowing all Braden had been through, Amy thought it even more important to keep the news from him than Ian.

The silence must have told him something was amiss. "Merry does the cooking, right?"

Shifting the rock around to suit her, as if fitting it just so was a matter of life and death, she bent to get another one. Neither she nor Meredith would lie if they were asked. But they didn't want the men to know yet. Meredith had felt better the last couple of days. A week from now, maybe two, she would be ready to announce her wonderful news.

Calming herself, Amy forged on, hoping Braden would forget her careless words. "I do want to help her, though."

She felt Braden studying her as she kept her back to him and busied herself with the smokehouse. Suddenly, Braden's big hands appeared beside her and picked up a rock.

Sighing with relief, Amy worked quickly, glad she'd fooled him but feeling guilty. They'd had such a nice moment together, and now her dishonesty had placed a barrier between them.

As they worked on the smokehouse, her mind went to her mother, who'd taught Amy the skill of building an *atx'aan hídi* to preserve their food, and from there her thoughts went to Papa.

"Braden, I want to go back to my father's house."

"I'm really sorry about your da." The dry scratch of stone on stone made a hushed backdrop to Braden's solemn voice.

Amy regretted that the laughter was gone.

"I haven't told you how sorry I am for your loss because. . . well, there hasn't been time." Braden's height made the stone structure go up faster. As the smokehouse wall grew higher, Amy began handing him rocks rather than nesting them herself, and the system worked smoothly.

Amy knew there'd been plenty of time for Braden to mention her loss. They'd been here nearly two weeks, and they'd eaten three meals a day together. But they'd avoided each other. The long journey here had forged a friendship between them that confused Amy. Worrying about her father and his home, and now caring for Meredith and three hungry men were all she could handle. An attraction to the kind man who had cared for her but still loved his wife, was a complication she didn't need.

For Braden's part, she knew he still mourned his wife. His perfect wife. He'd spoken of her a few times, how ladylike she was, how gracious and soft spoken. Amy glanced at the calluses on her hands and the tan she'd already gotten from working outside for long hours. Her Tlingit heritage showed far more since her return to Alaska. Relearning the ways her mother had taught her enhanced her resemblance to her native people. With a sad heart, she knew she looked and acted nothing like the woman Braden had loved and lost.

"It takes a lot of hard work to make a go of Alaska," she said quietly. "There is not a lot of time to visit."

"I think you're better off forgetting about the house. It's sold. I know you must miss your home."

A high scream overhead pulled their eyes upward. A golden

eagle swooped across the cloudless blue sky, its wings spread wide as it played on the cool spring air currents. The breeze ruffled the cedars surrounding Amy's smokehouse, creating the music of nature with their sway and the eagle cry. The white cap of a mountain peak soared above the tree tops.

Amy's throat swelled at the beauty all around her. She had missed her home. But her home was the land, not that cabin. She didn't want the building, only the information it contained. She couldn't rest peacefully until she knew what had happened to her father.

As another scream from the eagle reached her ears, she felt as if God spoke to her. " 'But they that wait upon the Lord shall renew their strength; they shall mount up with wings as eagles.' " Amy quoted. "My mother favored that verse mainly because of the beauty of the eagles that lived all around us. That verse always lifted my heart as surely as the wind lifts an eagle's wings."

Amy glanced at Braden. His shoulders stiffened. "You do not talk much of your faith, Braden. Can you find no comfort in knowing that your wife has gone home to God?"

Braden looked up from where he worked. "My wife is with God. I'm sure she's in a better place. But that doesn't leave any excuse for my making her life harder than it needed to be. I should have been stronger."

Stronger how? Amy held her tongue. *"Wait upon the Lord. . . . Mount up with wings as eagles."* A beautiful image. The wind seemed to whisper through the trees, *Patience, wait on the Lord.* In this one thing, questioning Braden, perhaps it would be better to wait. He seemed far from being ready to talk of his loss. But waiting for Braden's heart to heal was not the same as waiting to find the truth about her father. Braden needed time, but time was the enemy of the truth. Waiting might mean the man got away with murder.

Amy had cared for herself since the age of twelve and believed God wanted her to. So why did the Lord nudge her to wait? Did she hear God's voice carried on the wind or was it just her imagination? The Raffertys offered her safety and an easy life. But if she needed to face something hard, she'd just as soon get on with it. She turned back to the rock pile and selected the next stone.

"There is a hidden compartment in the mantel. It held Papa's important papers." Straightening with the next piece of granite, she added, "If he really sold the cabin, then he would have handed over the deed. But if—"

"Your home is gone." Braden laid his hand on her shoulder. "You need to accept that, lass."

Amy's jaw tightened. "Nobody *accepts* their father's un-explained death and the theft of their home. You haven't accepted your wife's death, have you?"

Braden took the load from her hands and rested it on the ever-narrowing chimney that had grown to chest level. "It's not about accepting. I—I just know God took her from me, and I want her back. If I'd taken better care of her, God would have blessed my efforts and let us be together for a long life. I failed. And now you want to risk confronting that man with his gun just to get a house back you don't need and you can't live in. Well, I'm not going to let you go."

"Not *let* me?" Amy clamped her lips tight and turned back to the smokehouse. She worked harder, wanting to keep her sharp words locked inside. Braden didn't deserve to be barked at. In his own overprotective way, he meant to be kind.

The smokehouse was soon done. Amy had left small, arched openings at each level. Now she knelt at the base and loaded the damp moss and green branches and wood chips. She found the match she'd tucked in the pocket of her gingham dress and carefully struck it on the stone. The matches were a wonderful convenience—though she certainly didn't need one to start a fire.

A pile of shredded bark resting on a larger slab of bark blazed to life, and Amy eased it into the base of the atx'aan hídi.

The sweet sound of crackling wood came from inside the smokehouse. The warm smell of cedar smoke tickled her nose. As the fire blazed inside the rounded opening, Amy used each level of the smokehouse, with its neat openings, to lay out her salmon.

Braden caught on quickly and worked at a different level so they wouldn't get in each other's way.

It only took moments for the blazing fire to die down and begin smoldering. Smoke billowed out of the hundreds of cracks of the chimney. They finished putting the salmon into the smoky chamber and stood back to keep from choking.

The sense of accomplishment eased Amy's temper, and she shared a smile with Braden. "This will burn for hours. I need to add wood twice a day. We will keep the fire going overnight. Tomorrow, about noon, this batch will be done, and I will take it out and add the salmon I spear today.

"Today?"

Amy nodded. "I need to get enough for the winter right now. It is easy when they are spawning. There are plenty of salmon in the river, of course. But my stream is better. And it needs to be done now. Later in the summer, I might sit all day and only spear enough food for a single meal. I will do that, of course, so we can eat fresh fish during the summer."

"Earlier, when I mentioned Merry doing all the cooking, you acted like something was wrong. What's going on?"

Amy had hoped he'd forgotten that blunder. But this talk of food had obviously reminded Braden. She toyed with a small rock, fitting it into an opening to keep a bit more of the smoke inside. The chimney wasn't meant to be tight. She fiddled with the rock to give herself time to think.

Braden pulled her hands away from the smokehouse and turned her to face him. "I asked if something was going on."

Amy studied her toes peeking out from beneath her brown calico dress, not a bit sure she could keep an innocent expression on her face. Suddenly he caught her upper arms in his hands and lifted her until she had to look at him. "What is it, Amy? Is Merry sick?"

Amy shook her head. She couldn't outright lie, and from his worried expression, she knew Braden wouldn't let the subject drop. "The smell of cooking meat makes her sick because. . . because. . ." Amy prayed that Meredith wouldn't be too upset with her. "She is expecting a baby."

"A baby?" A smile bloomed on his face. Then, as if the bloom were slashed off with a knife, his forehead furrowed, and the corners of his mouth turned down. Braden released her hands as if he'd found himself holding a rattlesnake. His jaw formed a taut, straight line; deep furrows showed on his brow, partly covered by his unruly red hair.

He stepped back from her. "No."

Amy felt the pain and fear rolling off Braden in waves. "She will be fine." She rested one hand on his wrist. "I know you lost your wife and you are worried for Merry, but babies are a blessing. She will be fine."

"You can't know that."

"She is a strong woman. There is nothing more natural than having a baby. God will take care of her."

"Like he took care of Maggie?" Braden shook off her touch and shoved both hands into his hair as he turned away.

Amy had lived with the Tlingit ways for too long to fear the birth of a baby. It was a reason for joy. Her mother had assisted whenever a baby came along, and Amy knew the way of bringing a child into the world. But how could she reassure Braden?

Amy knew the truth. If Braden didn't want to hear it, she couldn't force him. Speaking just above a whisper, she said, "Maggie's time to go home to God came. I know you miss her. You loved your wife and wanted that child, but God called them to Himself. To be angry at God for doing it makes no sense."

With a twist of guilt, Amy realized she'd been ignoring God's urging for patience. For a moment, she wondered if that also made no sense. But it wasn't the same thing. She accepted her father's death. She only wanted to see justice done; that bore no resemblance to anger with God.

"I've heard it all before." Braden dropped his hands to his sides, his fists clenched. He looked at Amy, his blue eyes smoldering like the stones behind them. "Why would God send a child only to take it away before it drew a single breath? Why would I hear Maggie's screams only to be useless as she lay and bled to death in my arms?"

"Oh, Braden." She laid one hand on his wrist, hurting for him. "I am so sorry. I did not know you went through all that."

He jerked his hand away as if she'd burned him. "Sorry for me? Maggie's the one who died. I don't deserve your sympathy. And I won't accept that as God's will. How can I? To accept it means God wanted to hurt me. What kind of God is that?"

"We cannot know the ways of God." Amy looked into pain that permeated the depths of Braden's heart. She remembered the bitter loneliness she'd felt when her mother had died. Nothing had come close to easing her pain except when her father held her. Despite the way Braden had rejected her touch, she couldn't stop herself from taking the few steps toward him and throwing her arms around him.

His hands went to her wrists behind his back as if he'd tear her loose. Then, with a sudden groan of pain, he released her wrists and pulled her hard against him.

Burying his face in her shoulder, he wept.

ten

Tears escaped as if a dam had burst when Braden felt Amy, solid and alive and strong in his arms. Her vitality and calm filled him with the courage to face the pain of Maggie's death. Until this minute, he'd clung to his anger and guilt, afraid of the tears as if once he began to cry he might never stop.

Vaguely, he felt Amy pat his back. He heard murmurs of comfort spoken so quietly he couldn't make them out. He thought she spoke of God, or maybe she spoke to God.

Braden knew a prayer was long overdue. *God, forgive me. I've blamed You. I've been angry at You. I'm so sorry.*

Braden remembered the words Ian had read to them one Sunday morning. *"But they that wait upon the Lord shall renew their strength; they shall mount up with wings as eagles; they shall run, and not be weary; and they shall walk, and not faint."*

"You're my strength, Braden."

But he hadn't been strong enough. Even though Maggie had demanded a lot of Braden, God had promised to renew his strength. *God, why didn't you make me strong enough?*

The awful sight of Maggie, bleeding, begging him to save her, dying in his arms faded into the memory of how she'd been before. She had a wonderful smile, though not so bright as Amy's. Amy's white teeth glowed out of her tanned face. Maggie had a gentle laugh, precious to Braden because he hadn't heard it often. Amy had at first appeared to have an overly serious nature. One of her gentle smiles had been rare indeed. Now on occasion, she shared a husky and generous laugh. He'd even heard her giggle with Meredith while they set the meal on the table. Once, under Tucker's merciless teasing, Amy had laughed so hard she'd held her stomach as if it hurt.

Braden realized he was comparing his wife to Amy. His tears stopped as soon as he realized the disloyalty of his thoughts. He felt compelled to say, "My Maggie was a gracious, gentle lady. Aye, she had the manners and temperament of an angel."

Braden thought of a few times Maggie hadn't been so sweet. She didn't lose her temper, but she did complain and gave way to tears and long, pouting silences. Braden had learned to give her what she wanted to keep peace in his home.

Amy had lost her father; she'd been left homeless with only a stranger to care for her. She'd been exhausted from the trip. But she'd handled it all. She'd fought her way through the loss, the exhaustion, and the fear. She'd squared her shoulders and taken on the household so Meredith could rest. And she'd done it quietly.

Even Meredith, tired out from the baby growing inside her, hadn't whined and demanded Ian stay in the house as Maggie had with Braden. Meredith had accepted Amy's help out of necessity but kept working. She'd sewn three shirts this week out of the fabric Ma had sent, one for each of the men. Braden had seen no new clothing for Meredith or Amy as of yet.

Braden remembered how Maggie needed to be complimented for things. He'd loved to put that glow in her eyes when she'd show him a shirt she'd mended or a cake she'd baked. Even while he did it, Braden thought of his mother baking daily for the large household, gardening, canning, and cleaning all day. Ma sewed or knit in the evening, her hands never idle, her thoughts always on what came next and who needed her help.

Amy reminded Braden of his mother, a hard worker with no need for thanks because she saw herself as part of the family and worked to make the family run smoothly. Ma and Da had trained their young'uns to say please and thank you, but no one did their work for the thanks they earned with it. Not his mother, not Amy, not Meredith, only Maggie.

Braden realized he still held Amy. It had felt so natural he'd kept hanging on. He stepped out of Amy's arms, pulling away so abruptly that she stumbled toward him when she didn't let go quickly enough. He dashed his shirt sleeve across his eyes.

He saw the confusion in her eyes and dropped his gaze to her soft lips. He thought of the Northern Lights in the sky when they were together on the trip up here. He'd been drawn to her then, and the very idea had shocked him. Now he wanted to pull her close. He wanted her warmth and strength not just for a day but forever. Braden shoved his hands in his pockets to stop himself from reaching for her. The pain of losing Maggie was too fresh; caring for another woman felt like a betrayal. He had to say something to rebuild the wall he needed to protect his heart.

"There's no room in a family for lies and secrets." His tone shocked him. The rough edge of it calling Amy a liar. "If you women don't tell Ian the truth, I will."

He found safety in his anger and looked at the little woman who'd just built a smokehouse and had plans that would feed the family for the winter. Amy had gone fishing yesterday, leaving Meredith home alone all day. Now here she planned to do it again. Maggie would never have done that. Maggie would have stayed to the house where she belonged.

Glaring, his temper came rapidly to a boil to cover his guilt. "If you're going to go off on your own and leave Merry, you'd better tell us so someone can be there in case she needs help."

Amy's jaw dropped. He saw the tracks of tears cutting through her grubby face, tears she'd cried for him. She'd worked up a sweat building the chimney, then apparently scratched her nose and cheeks with dirty hands.

Maggie kept herself neat and clean.

"Braden, what is wrong?" Amy's kindness only made him more furious. He felt like a polar bear, lashing out at her for no reason except his own bad temper. But he couldn't stop.

"Are you going to keep lying to Ian or not?"

"We did not lie. We just—"

"Just didn't tell the truth." Guilt rode him like the gnawing hunger of an empty belly after a long winter's hibernation. "Don't dress it up fancy to make excuses for yourself. That makes you a liar."

Amy's head jerked back as if she'd been slapped.

Braden had to lock his muscles in place to keep from reaching for her and telling her she was wonderful, beautiful, brave, and strong.

Amy met his eyes, as if she accepted his condemnation and believed every word. "I—I will tell Merry. Now that you know, she will need to tell Ian, of course. I think we should let her be the one to tell him."

Braden held her gaze for a moment longer. Then with a single nod of his chin, he said, "Do it before the end of the noon meal, or I will."

He turned and plunged into the woods, afraid to be near her for another second.

৵

Amy sank onto the nearest rock. What had happened? One second she'd been in Braden's arms, comforting him, feeling closer to him than she ever had to another human being. The next, he'd been calling her a liar and threatening her if she didn't admit everything to Ian.

She should never have hugged him. The mission teachers had told her about a woman's proper demeanor. She'd shocked Braden and once again reminded him of how poorly she compared to the refined wife he'd lost.

A gust of wind carried a thick blanket of fish-flavored smoke over her, setting her to coughing. If it hadn't been for that, she might have sat on that rock forever.

The smoke reminded her of dinner, and, fighting back tears of shame for the way she'd flaunted herself at Braden, she hurried toward the house. She needed to give Meredith a few minutes to prepare herself before Ian got home.

She strode toward the cabin, her mind jumping around like a speared salmon fighting its fate. A sudden crackling in the brush drew her attention. She turned to face the noise, resting her hand on the hilt of her knife, tucked in its scabbard and tied around her waist with a thin leather belt. She always carried it in case she needed to cut saplings or dig for roots.

Ian and Tucker had warned her that they'd seen the white fur of a polar bear and its tracks in the woods, but not this near. She knew how hungry the huge animals were in the spring. The smell of smoking salmon would draw them. That's why she'd used the heavy rocks to build the smokehouse, rather than just hang them over an open fire. Keeping a watchful eye on the woods, she listened for the heavy breathing of a bear, watched for a flash of white fur against the brown of the trees and the green of the cedar branches.

She heard something more but it didn't sound like a bear, more like a footstep. Human. A cold chill raced up her spine as she backed away from the thick undergrowth and remembered the menace of those soft footfalls that late night aboard the *Northward* and how she'd never stayed on the deck alone again. She pulled her knife. "Who is there?"

She continued backing away, keeping her eyes open, listening for movement that meant someone circled her. She heard nothing. As soon as she put enough paces between her and that thicket, she pivoted and raced for the cabin.

By the time she got to the house, she had begun to doubt the strange flash of fear. Feeling foolish for racing through the woods, she slowed her steps and tried to steady her breathing. Running a hand through the wisps of black hair that had escaped her braid, she tidied herself. No sense frightening Meredith just because Amy jumped at her own shadow. With a shake of her head, Amy entered the cabin to see Meredith sitting on Ian's lap.

They were both grinning.

Amy forgot all about that strange moment in the woods. "You told him."

Meredith nodded. Ian jumped from the chair with Meredith still in his arms and whooped, twirling her around in the air.

Amy stepped back so she wouldn't get plowed over in the tiny cabin, laughing at Ian's antics.

"Ian, stop. I'm going to throw up." Meredith slapped at his shoulder, but then she went back to holding him tight. She didn't look sick. She looked wonderful. Amy saw none of the greenish hue to her skin. Her eyes glowed with joy, her cheeks were flushed pink from laughter, and her lips were slightly swollen, no doubt from Ian's kisses.

"Well, good," Amy said, "because Braden found out today. He insisted that we tell Ian. . . *today*."

Meredith, perched in her husband's arms, arched a brow at Amy. "You talked with Braden this morning?"

"Yes." Amy refused to say more despite Meredith's open curiosity. "Ian, take your wife outside so I can cook some dinner. This cabin is not big enough for me and a dancing couple."

"I'm feeling better." Meredith squeezed Ian's neck until he grunted. "I think I could help cook today."

"Not right now." Amy shook her head. "I think you need to go and spend a few minutes with your husband. You can try cooking tonight."

Ian smiled, whirled Meredith one more time, then swept toward the door with his wife still in his arms.

Amy jumped out of the way, laughing at Ian's nonsense. She turned to watch them go and saw Braden standing at the edge of the clearing. Ian and Meredith didn't see him; they were too caught up in their own joy. Could it have been Braden she'd heard in the woods? Would he have kept quiet if she'd come upon him, rather than speak to her, even after he'd seen her fear?

With his heart in his eyes, Braden watched his brother and Meredith. The grief cut lines into the corners of his mouth and deepened the lines in his forehead.

The happy couple vanished into the woods, and Braden turned to Amy.

Anger replaced grief, and even from this distance, she could see the accusation, as if she'd betrayed him somehow. The betrayal boiled down to Amy being alive while his beloved Maggie was dead.

I am in love with him.

From out of nowhere, the knowledge swept over her as powerfully as an avalanche. His expression couldn't have hurt as much as it did for any other reason. At that moment, she'd have done anything to take away his pain, even given up her life in exchange for his Maggie's if God granted her the power to make such a trade.

Her eyes held Braden's. Then, as if he couldn't bear the sight of her a moment longer, he turned away and disappeared into the trees in the opposite direction his brother and sister-in-law had gone.

❧

Amy fed the family and, with some argument, settled Meredith in for an afternoon nap. After the excitement of telling Ian her news, she looked exhausted. Meredith protested, but she fell asleep almost before Amy left the room.

Amy tended the fire in her smokehouse, then set off through the woods. She planned to haul home a much larger catch today. Knowing she had the smokehouse to build first, she hadn't taken the time to carry more salmon home yesterday. Settling into the long, silent strides her father had taught her when he took her along to his trap lines, she covered a mile and had two more to go. She moved easily up the rugged mountain, reveling in the beauty of her home.

She might not have come after the uncomfortable moment in the woods earlier if she hadn't convinced herself the noises, assuming they were human, were from Braden sulking. That stopped her from mentioning the incident at the table while they ate, too. Although she should have said something, the meal was a joyful one with Meredith and Ian elated over their news, and it had been easy to keep her vague fears to herself.

A still, small voice whispered to her to wait, to take someone along, to not strike out alone in the woods. The only thing that gave her pause was leaving Meredith alone. But Ian and Tucker had always left Meredith when they went to the mines, so they must believe it to be safe. Amy ignored her doubts in favor of action.

Her mind firmly on Braden and the way he'd held her and then pushed her away, she only distantly noticed the terrain. She'd climbed this path before, after all. She reached the summit of the modest mountain that separated her from the rich salmon run. She paused at the top, drinking in the hundreds of scenic peaks that made this look like a footstool for God's grand throne. The small mountain she stood on wasn't even high enough to be capped with snow. She followed a trail that skirted a cedar stand on her right hand and on her left dropped away in a sheer fall.

Only a few stunted trees clung to the rugged mountainside.

A lip of the trail stuck out far enough that the cliff face wasn't visible for nearly a hundred feet. She looked over the edge and saw, far below, the silver waters of the stream she sought.

Beautiful—the rushing waters audible even from this high, the soft hush of the wind flowing over her like the breath of God. Sighing, inhaling the cold crisp air, she turned to head down.

Swift footfalls sounded behind her.

With only seconds to react, Amy whirled to face the direction of the running steps, but hard hands caught her before she could turn fully around. A vicious shove launched her into midair. As she fell, cruel, satisfied laughter rang in her ears. Laughter she now remembered. Laughter she'd heard in Seattle as she'd fallen under the hooves of a charging horse.

eleven

Amy twisted and clawed at the cliff. A stunted tree grew out of the rock. Her chest slammed into it. The tree crackled, and the limbs cut her hands as she scrabbled for a hold. The impact jerked her fingers free, and she fell again.

A protruding rock jabbed her belly. Amy grunted at the blow, fighting to draw a breath. She hung draped over the rock, head and feet hanging down. The world swayed. The narrow rock under her belly gave her no room to balance. She began to slide feet first off the ledge. She grabbed at the jagged wall beside her, shredding her palm.

Her gaze darted around. A little crack in the rock formed a *V*. Amy's left hand clawed at the fissure. Her other arm swung in a wild arc over the long drop.

Her battered fingers slipped from the niche. She clenched her fist and punched it into the fissure, ripping flesh. Her weight locked her fist in the narrow opening. The protruding rock now pressed against her face.

Her body hung, suspended from one arm, wrenching her shoulder. For a sickening second, only that tremulous fist stood between her and death. Her strength wouldn't have held her. The rock pinched her fist tight, trapping her, saving her.

Amy turned her face away from the scraping rock and looked down. Below her kicking, dangling feet was a sheer drop of a hundred feet. Dizziness swept over her. Nausea twisted her stomach. She wrenched her head sideways to block her vision, choosing to focus on the rough rock scraping her cheek rather than the sickening knowledge of just how far she'd fall if her hand gave way.

With her other hand, she found a lip on the protruding rock and grabbed hold.

She fought her way back onto the tiny ledge. Once steady, she realized the rock she'd hit cut back into the cliff a few inches. Sliding into the indentation, she found a secure spot.

Careful not to lose her balance, she turned her back to the cliff and pressed against the rocks. Once tucked into the little cleft, she worked her hand free of the crack that had saved her. Looking up, she saw the cliff overhang.

Her stomach burned from the blow against the ledge. Blood streamed off her knuckles, and both her palms bled from frantically clinging to the stunted tree. Her blunt nails were torn and bleeding. Pain radiated from her face where it had ground against stone. When she gingerly touched her throbbing cheek, her fingertips came away stained scarlet with blood. Her back, undamaged in the fall, burned with the feel of shoving hands.

Someone had tried to kill her. A wave of dizziness almost upset her balance, and she forced her mind to remain clear. She had to think.

Wait on the Lord.

God chided her for striking out on her own after the meal. Or did He mean that she should wait now? Don't climb to safety. Wait for help.

She decided it meant the first. God had tried to warn her that the woods held danger for her. Well, she knew now, and she'd be careful. *I'm sorry I didn't listen, Lord.*

She turned her eyes upward to see if she could climb out.

Wait on the Lord.

Perhaps she would rest up for a few minutes.

Catching her breath, she listened for any sound from above.

Never one to ignore hard facts,. she faced the truth. She had no doubt that shove was a deliberate murder attempt. With shocking clarity, she realized someone had tried to kill her in Seattle, also. And maybe on the boat that night she'd been alone on the deck and that day by the railing. And someone had been lurking in the woods near her smokehouse. She wondered if Braden's presence had headed off an attack earlier.

Who?

She thought of the man who'd come to her father's door. Would that man silence the only person on earth who might dispute his claim?

There had been others on the ship who'd made her uncomfortable. Darnell Thompson, with his too-watchful eyes, had been close that day at the railing. Had he hoped for one last chance to kill her?

What about the oily little Barnabas Stucky?

Both men had claimed to be stampeders. Both had offered to accompany her home. No gold miner on his way to the Klondike took a side trip to go sightseeing. Not even a woman in a nearly all-male world could turn those madmen aside.

Amy sat and thought it through as her breathing steadied and the worst of the pain eased from her hands. When she had quit trembling, she began to assess her situation.

Studying the sheer wall below her, she knew going down was impossible. Amy had scampered around mountains many times in her childhood. She tried to pick out footholds and handholds in the rock face and found none.

Above her, Amy could see a way, precarious but possible for about half the distance to the top. After that, the cliff curved out of sight for a few feet before ending at the overhang. Her climb might lead her all the way up or leave her stranded, possibly unable to go back, hanging over thin air.

But if she did get to the top, what awaited her? Someone who even now had noticed that she'd stopped her headlong fall to death? Or had he shoved her and run like a sneaking coward who would attack a woman from behind?

Amy sat quietly, listening. She'd been preoccupied as she'd walked, a foolish mistake that she'd have never made before her years in Washington. But even distracted, she'd have noticed any blatant sounds. That meant whoever had pushed her knew the woods.

And that made him smart enough to wait quietly and make sure he finished his job.

Amy looked at the sun still high in the sky. She knew the patience of the north country. She knew what it meant to out-wait a stalking cougar or a hungry bear. This ledge twenty feet down a cliff felt safe. For now, maybe the safest place between here and the Raffertys. She'd stay.

Wait on the Lord.

For now, she'd wait.

ta

"Honey, what are you doing out here?"

At the sound of Ian's worried voice, Braden turned from the rock he chiseled. Meredith stood near their most recent digging, her trim body silhouetted against the sunlight. Her shoulders rose and fell as she panted.

Ian and Tucker had worked their way through solid stone during the last year. Braden had already found a couple of thin streaks of the golden wealth that God had created and sewn into the fabric of the earth. None of the streaks went deep.

He couldn't see his sister-in-law's face, but he could feel her tension. He dropped his pick and heard two other metallic clangs from Tucker and Ian as they advanced on Meredith.

Ian got there first. Braden and Tucker were a step behind.

"Amy's never come back." Meredith flung herself into Ian's arms. "I should have waited, but I've just got this terrible feeling. She promised to be back in time to start dinner. I told her I'd do it, but she insisted, and she's never failed to keep her word."

Ian lifted his wife, her feet dangling above the ground, and carried her out of the mine. He brushed the wisps of brown hair off her flushed cheeks.

"You shouldn't have hiked all the way up here."

Ian, Meredith, and Tucker all turned on Braden when he spoke.

Worry creased Ian's forehead as he turned back to his wife. "Are you all right?"

"I just couldn't wait. I feel fine. I was careful." Meredith turned away from Ian, who kept his hands around her waist. Her eyes blazed at Braden until he could feel the heat.

"I couldn't sit at home *when I'm fine* while Amy might be in danger."

Braden arched a brow at Meredith's fierce strength, so different than anything he'd known with Maggie. Another pang of guilt hit him as he compared Maggie to another woman and found his wife wanting. Not everyone was strong. Not everyone had what it took to tackle an unsettled land. That wasn't Maggie's fault.

Clenching his jaw to keep from defending Maggie when no one here had said a word against her, Braden nodded. "No, of course you couldn't."

"Where did she go?" Tucker stepped past Braden and studied his twin. He pulled a handkerchief out of his hip pocket and mopped Meredith's sweaty, dirt-streaked face. The walk up here was strenuous.

Braden's stomach clenched in fear for Meredith's baby—and for Amy. Meredith spoke the truth about Amy's dependability.

Something had happened to her. Why had he let her set off in the wilderness? What if that polar bear had attacked her?

Braden fought down his growing panic. "She said she needed more salmon. She mentioned the spawning bed. Where is that?"

Tucker and Ian exchanged a glance over Meredith's head. Ian looked at Braden. "I don't know. The few salmon we catch come from the Skaguay River. The two of you talked about the smokehouse, but she never said where exactly she'd caught the fish.

Meredith spun around to face Ian. "You can find her. You can track her down and bring her home."

Braden remembered his brother in the woods when they were young. He'd moved with the silence of a cloud of smoke. He'd made a game of sneaking up on wild animals.

"Yes," Braden said, "you can do this, Ian."

Ian looked at Tucker. "I want you to walk down to the cabin slowly with Meredith. Make sure she doesn't overdo it."

"Ian, I'm fine!" Meredith clenched her fists.

Ian rested a hand on her cheek. "I know you are, honey. But let Tucker take care of you, please. Braden and I are going after Amy, and we're going fast. That means I'm leaving you behind, and it'll take a load off my mind if I know you're being easy on yourself."

He lowered his hand from her cheek to her stomach. "You told me you get dizzy sometimes. That's a mighty serious business when you're walking alone with no one to catch you if you fall. Let Tucker get you home safe. Please."

Meredith rested her hand on top of Ian's. To Braden it looked like the two of them were holding their unborn child. The sight warmed his heart and for once he felt no pain when he thought of a baby.

Meredith nodded. "I'll behave." She reached up and gave

Ian a quick kiss on the cheek. "Now get out of here and find Amy. If I lose that woman, I don't know what I'll do." She said it lightly, but there was nothing humorous about a missing woman in the wilderness.

Braden didn't know what he'd do, either.

Ian cut his gaze to Braden. "Let's get moving."

Ian took off down the mountain at a near run with Braden right on his heels.

In the time it took Braden to load both rifles, Ian had found Amy's tracks heading straight up the mountain, away from the river.

"What salmon live up there?" Braden muttered.

"There's a stream that empties into the river. It winds around like crazy, and I've never followed it. I'll bet she's heading for that. Climbing up and down this mountain will be shorter than going around, I'm figuring."

Silently they fell into step, Ian in the lead. He passed through a thick patch of trees and dropped to the ground so suddenly Braden almost tripped over him.

"This is an old game trail. I've never noticed it before. How did she find it so fast?"

Braden could see Amy's footprints heading uphill.

Ian pointed. "You can see she went up and came back down yesterday. But there's no sign of her returning today." Ian looked up through the spruce and cedars grown close together, clinging as if by a miracle to the rocky ground. Shrubs tangled together, mixing with the scent of pine and showing off their summer finery of berries and flowers, sometimes guarded by wicked thorns. Heavy branches drooped across the trail.

Ian set off, pushing through the dense foliage, following her trail easily. She'd moved quickly, her strides long. The rocky soil gave way to solid rock, and a few yards after that the trail split. One side went up, the other down.

Ian crouched to study the ground. He rose and went a few long strides up the slope, then came back to brush his fingers over the lower route. Hunkered down to touch the plants along the trail, he turned at last to Braden. "I can't tell which way she went. There's no sign of a footprint on the stone. This could be the way down to the stream. I'll follow this one." Ian gave the plant one more look as if he could hear it speaking and was listening for Amy's route. Then he pointed at the upward trail. "You see if you can find any tracks that way."

"What if the trail divides again?" It could divide a hundred times, and they could be days exploring all the possibilities.

Ian shook his head. "Let's don't borrow trouble."

Braden nodded, then headed up, tension growing in his stomach. Amy was now long overdue. She'd have been on time, toting those blasted fish, and Braden knew it. The stone path stretched ahead relentlessly, as if a thousand years of winter winds had scrubbed every breath of soil from its surface, leaving no chance for a single footprint. He could find no evidence Amy had come this way.

He reached the peak and stopped at the edge of a cliff to look down on the stream far below. He could hear the rushing water. Did that mean she'd taken this path? Or was it the one Ian had followed?

The soaring view, breathtaking in its beauty, made Braden feel closer to God than he had since Maggie died.

"God, where is she?" He prayed aloud.

"Braden, is that you?"

Braden gasped at the voice coming from under his feet and jumped backward. Then he dropped to his knees and leaned out over the edge of the cliff.

"Be careful!" She sounded exasperated. "There isn't room for anyone else down here."

Despite his shock, Braden grinned. "You sound okay." He lay on his stomach and scooted out far enough so that he could look around a scrub cedar and see Amy looking up, her expression disgruntled as if she wondered what took him so long.

twelve

"What in the world took you so long?" Amy began her cautious ascent, ignoring her shredded hands, dried blood, throbbing skin. She'd been planning to climb up as soon as someone came to find her. After just a couple of months with the Raffertys, she knew to expect them, and she feared facing whoever had pushed her, so she'd waited. Yes, for once she'd waited. She breathed a prayer of thanksgiving for Braden's presence.

She reached the curve in the rock face and got a firm grasp on the stunted tree. Pulling herself up to use it for a foothold, she stopped. With five feet from her outstretched hand to the top, there wasn't a handhold in sight. Her stomach twisted as she thought of being stranded on this sheer rock with her battered hands, trying to back up. The places she'd found to hold were little more than half-inch wide ledges in the rough stone and then this tree with its rough bark and piercing needles. Now, instead of the mortal danger she would have faced had she refused to wait, she had Braden.

He reached for her. She reached back. Their hands met in the middle and locked together. The pain of his solid grip on her battered hand told her she was alive and safe. She met his gaze and had no fear of letting go of her last anchor. Braden would hang on. He'd pull her to safety.

It struck her again just as it had earlier. Yes, she loved him. And he was a fine man, worthy of her love. It was she who didn't measure up. She could work from sun to sun—and that said a lot in an Alaskan June—but she'd never be the genteel lady who'd won his heart. Amy felt sure that the harder she worked, the more she underlined her unfitness for him.

Braden pulled her up, catching her other arm when it came within reach. Once he had her securely, he slid his arm around her waist and tugged, rearing back on his knees as she came over the ledge. They tumbled onto the trail together. Braden jumped to his feet. He stayed close, as if ready to grab her should she fall back over the cliff.

Amy climbed more slowly upright, every joint in her body aching. Braden kept a steady hand on her arm. They looked over the dead drop, then Amy turned away, shaken to think how close she'd come to dying.

"Thank God, you're all right." Braden's heartfelt words brought her head up. His eyes skimmed over her bruised, bleeding face; then he clamped one hard hand on her waist and pulled her into his arms.

"You could have died." Braden's head lowered. "I could have lost you."

Their lips met.

Braden broke the kiss. Amy's eyes flickered open as Braden stepped away, turning toward the cliff. He rubbed the back of his neck with one hand and stared into space. Where a moment ago, she'd been warm, now the cool, dry Alaskan air chilled her lips.

Amy knew what would come next. Regret. A list of her inadequacies—a list of Maggie's virtues. She spoke before he could.

"Do not touch me again."

Braden's head rose, and his eyebrows arched. "I–I won't. I'm sorry."

Regret. Already. Now here came a list of her inadequacies. She headed him off. "Fine. As long as we are clear."

Amy crossed her arms. "Now what are we going to do about this?"

Braden's eyes dropped to her lips.

"Not that!" Amy snapped.

Braden looked her in the eye, his face flushed.

"What are we going to do about the man who pushed me off that cliff?"

"What?" Braden pushed his battered Stetson back.

"I stayed down there because I feared he might still be here."

"He?"

"The man who pushed me off the cliff." Amy looked around. She'd be on her guard now like she should have been all along. She was lucky she had survived to be more careful.

"A man pushed you off the cliff?" Braden looked around.

"Did you think I fell? Do you believe I am a clumsy city woman who trips over her own feet?"

"Uh, yes, I mean, no, not clumsy," Braden said. "But you're from the city after all."

"I am from Alaska. This is my home. I am as sure-footed as a bighorn sheep, and I do *not* trip over the side of a cliff by accident." Amy clenched her jaw and fists in the same breath and turned away from him. She forced herself to be practical. Looking for tracks, she saw the solid rock underfoot. There'd be no tracks. Even off the trail, the shrubs grew out of tumbled rock.

"How long ago did this happen?" Braden's sharp, wary voice got her attention.

"I have been on that ledge for at least four hours."

"Four hours?" His brows slammed together as he studied her scraped face. "How did you hold on so long?"

"What choice did I have?"

He frowned, then looked into the underbrush, going straight to the most obvious hiding place. "No tracks. Whoever did it picked the perfect spot."

Amy had already learned of Ian's skill in the wilderness. But Braden also looked comfortable studying the trail, searching for signs left behind by the attacker. She watched him run his hand over the ground as if he could feel the presence of someone from hours ago. Father had tracked like that.

Braden turned to Amy. "What did he look like?"

"I did not see him. I just heard someone run up behind me. Then he pushed." *And laughed like in Seattle.* She opened her mouth to tell Braden this wasn't the first attack.

"He? You saw a man?"

"No, I just said I did not see anyone."

Braden crossed his arms. "Then how do you know a man pushed you?"

"Because. . .because. . ." Amy faltered.

Braden's eyes narrowed.

"Because I suspect I was pushed by the man who stole my father's cabin."

Braden shook his head as if her answer disgusted him. "You're obsessed with your father's cabin."

"My obsession did not push me over that cliff."

Braden fell silent. Amy didn't like the look in his eyes.

Braden looked down at her hands and reached for them. "You're hurt."

She saw her palms, scraped raw. He turned them over, revealing several bleeding fingernails broken below the quick. Next his eyes focused on her face. "You're scraped here, too." He touched her cheek with a callused hand.

The teachers at the mission had warned her to hold herself apart from men, and she always had. Now Braden's gentle touch only brought pain because she knew he had judged her unworthy. She enjoyed the touch even as she knew she should push him away.

"We need to get you home. Can you walk?" Braden slid

one arm around her waist as if he planned to pick her up and carry her.

Hurt by his kindness when she knew it carried no affection, Amy stepped out of his reach. "I have been sitting all after-noon. I am rested as a bear awakened from his winter sleep by the chinook. What about the man who pushed me?" Amy started down the trail.

Braden jogged to catch up with her. "You're sure you were pushed?"

Amy stopped so suddenly Braden plowed into her back. She stumbled from the impact, and Braden caught her arm to steady her. She shook off his hand. "What do you mean, am I sure?"

Braden's fair skin turned pink, and he seemed very in-terested in the rock he kicked under his toe. "It's just that, well. . .you didn't really see anybody. Maybe you slipped, or maybe a branch fell out of a tree and hit—"

"What branch?" Amy turned back to the site where she'd fallen. "Would it not be lying there if it fell out of a tree and hit me?"

"Not if it fell over the cliff, too."

Speechless, Amy stared at Braden until finally the silence brought his head up. Once he looked at her, she asked rigidly, "Do you think I am a liar? You called me such this morning."

Braden shook his head until the red curls peeking out from under his hat danced. "I didn't say you lied."

"Then you think I am stupid."

"Amy, I. . ." Braden pulled his Stetson off and slid the brim around and around through his fingers.

"Do branches sound like running feet?" She slugged him in the shoulder, and he looked up.

"You never said anything about running feet."

"I did not know I stood in front of a judge giving testimony.

I thought I spoke to a friend who had some. . ." Her voice broke. Shocked at her weakness, she cleared her throat and went on. "Some respect for me."

"Now, you know I respect you. I saw that smokehouse you built."

Amy's eyes narrowed. "And you came running over to help me as if I were some fragile flower about to be crushed under the stones, even though I had obviously already built most of it alone."

"I just thought it looked like. . .like. . ." He went back to playing with his hat.

"Like hard work?" She slapped the hat out of his hands and only through sheer strength of will kept herself from stomping the crown into the stone path when it hit the ground at her feet. "Is that what you were going to say? You did not think I would want to do any hard work? As if I am lazy?"

"No." He looked up from his hat, glaring at her. "That's not what I meant. It's just hard. It's not woman's work. I didn't mean no offense."

"You call me a clumsy—"

"I didn't."

"Stupid—"

"You're not stupid."

"Lazy—"

"You work hard. I never said—"

"Liar."

"Well, you should have told Ian—"

"Is that about it? Perhaps you would toss me back over the cliff before my inferiority destroys your family."

"Now, Amy lass, don't be—"

"Let me tell you something about women's work, you stampeding *g'oon* hunter."

"Stampeding what?"

Amy might not have said it if she hadn't been so insulted. "*G'oon*. It means gold. You're one of the stampeders, are you not? One of the crazy men invading my beautiful Tlingit land for that golden rock."

"Your Clink It land?" He pronounced the word in a clumsy fashion. "What does that mean?"

"It means while you are calling me clumsy and lazy and stupid and a liar—"

"I did *not* say you were—"

"I am born to this land. I have learned how to find the true wealth in it without tearing out its heart with a pickax. My mother was a Tlingit."

"A what?"

Amy jammed her fisted hands on her hips and flinched when her scraped palms protested.

Braden caught one of her hands, and she wrenched it away. "One of the native people who lived for centuries in harmony with the snow and darkness before you came with your big steamer ships and soft ways."

"Soft ways?" Braden scooped up his hat and clapped it on his head. Dust puffed out from the brim.

"And I learned how to live in Alaska from her and my Russian father. Each of them alone is stronger than all you Raffertys put together."

Braden narrowed his eyes. "Y—your mother was an Eskimo?"

Amy remembered as she saw Braden's strange expression that her father had warned her people would treat her oddly if she told them of her native and Russian blood. Amy crossed her arms. Well, now came her chance to see how Braden reacted. This was his test, not hers.

"My mother is half Tlingit, I am one quarter. We're not *Eskimos*. That is a word your people use for all of us because you are too lazy to learn who we are, even while you insist there is a difference between your Irish, your Scots, your English, your Swedes, and your Germans. There are dozens of different groups up here. I am from the Tlingit nation. I know rugged land. I know narrow mountain passages. I know the difference between a falling branch and a running man."

Braden shook his head. "Then why haven't you said anything before? I mean, you said you grew up here, but I had no idea your roots went so deep."

"My name is Amaruq Simonovich. My father is a Russian fur trader, not a man to die easily. Not a man to sell a cabin he does not own. An old friend gave over the lovely spot out of the wind to my father. Papa comes and goes following the fur seasons. He has lived in that cabin for more than twenty years, but it is not his to sell. It is only his to live in."

"Amaruq? I heard Wily call you that, but I thought I'd just misunderstood. Then Amy—"

"My father wished to have me live as an American in Seattle."

"You *are* an American," Braden said indignantly.

"Father feared that I would be treated poorly as both a Tlingit and a Russian. So I abided by his wishes. But I am proud of my heritage, and I know this land. And I never want to speak to you again."

Amy whirled and charged down the trail. She nearly reached the bottom before Braden caught up with her and grabbed her arm.

"Listen, if you really think a man pushed you off that cliff. . ."

Amy jerked her arm loose and jammed her elbow into Braden's gut. It was like hitting iron. He had the nerve to smile as he caught hold of her again.

She defiantly tilted her chin.

Speaking as if he were addressing a two-year-old, he said,

"If someone pushed you off a cliff, you'd better not go running away on your own."

"I would rather—"

"If you're tellin' the truth. . ." Braden cut her off, his good humor evaporating. "Then stay with me." His eyes challenged her.

To dash past him back to the cabin would be to admit no danger existed. She thought of those pounding footsteps, and a shiver ran down her spine. She knew Braden felt it because his grip softened. He rubbed the length of her upper arm as if to warm her.

While she wanted to defy him, it *was* foolish to go off alone. Should she tell Braden her suspicions about what happened in Seattle? He'd just think she imagined that, too. Why not? She'd believed it an accident until just hours ago. That uncomfortable moment on the boat was even more vague.

It was foolish to go off alone earlier. Especially after I sensed someone watching me. Wait on the Lord.

Amy wanted to scream. She didn't want to wait on anyone. Not Braden, not God, and not the man who had attacked her. She pictured the cruel, bloodshot eyes of the man in her father's home. She wanted action. She wanted to charge straight for her father's cabin and force a confession out of that man.

She turned and stood at Braden's side like a well-trained dog. "You are right. It would be foolish. I will stay beside you as we go back, and then we will plan together how to oust this evil man from my home."

"The cabin again. What about us? What about Merry? We need you here. What good is a cabin goin' to do you all alone in the wilderness? You can't live there."

"Of course I can." She wrenched her arm away from his tender touch.

"But why would you? That's no life, one woman alone. Why not stay here with us?"

"It is not the cabin I care about; it is justice for my father I seek. That man most likely killed him. That is not something I will forget, especially since the same man is trying to kill me."

"If he is."

They stared at each other. Amy saw the stubborn line of Braden's jaw and knew he'd never help her, never see justice done. God wanted her to wait. Now Braden wanted her to wait. She couldn't do it.

"Ian should be meeting us down lower." Braden nodded toward the trail. "He took another path."

"That one leads into a ravine cut by a spring. It empties into this spring a long way to the south. You can get to the salmon beds from there, but my way is quicker."

"Now, tell me again how you know someone pushed you."

Amy retold her story, more carefully this time, including every detail. She even told Braden about the noise she'd heard earlier in the woods. As they walked, Amy's tension eased, and she felt the safety of a strong man at her side. It reminded her of her father and how he'd always cherished her.

Looking sideways at Braden, she said, "My mother's name was Yéil; it means raven, a sacred creature to my people. My mother and her village became Christians, but the old names are still special to them, and they often name a child after animals. My name, *Amaruq*, means wolf."

"Now that you say it, I can believe that you're an Eskimo."

Amy arched a brow.

"I mean a Clink It," Braden added with a faint blush. "But brown hair and brown eyes are common."

"Mother was a half-blood Tlingit raised in a Tlingit village and wise in their ways. My father is Petrov Simonovich, a Russian fur trader, born and raised in Alaska. They were both strong people from races suited to the cold, dark land." Amy crossed her arms and looked at Braden. "I have inherited their strength."

"You were barely surviving on that boat."

"That is because of an accident in Seattle." She clenched her jaw to keep from adding her suspicions to her story. "Part of the reason I decided to come home was the frantic pace of the city. Also, I could not support myself after my injuries. And I—" Amy stopped, then gathered her composure. "I missed my father. I had not heard from him in a long time. I needed to make sure he was all right."

Braden, his stride shortened out of concern for her, turned as they walked together. Amy saw him study her in the spring sunlight dappled by the hardy cedars and slender spruce that lined the narrow game trail, barely wide enough for two people. The sun sank lower in the sky, but hours of daylight remained.

"Amaruq, huh?" He grinned at her.

Amy tried to remember why her father thought it important to keep her heritage private.

"Amaruq Simonovich. Well, I guess you being here makes more sense than an Irish farmer."

Amy managed a smile. "A lot more sense."

Braden smiled, then laughed. Ian appeared from a little side trail and gave Amy a startled look.

"I am fine." Her mouth spoke the words, but her heart knew the truth. No one was fine who had someone trying to kill them.

thirteen

"Someone tried to kill you?" Meredith clutched Amy as if she were hanging off a cliff right that very minute.

Tucker jumped from his seat at the table, knocking his chair over. His eyes were wary, his body tense, coiled for action as if the attacker might come into the room at any moment.

Amy decided someone needed to build sturdier furniture for this household, and she was just the one to do it.

She saw Ian's eyes darken with worry as he hurried to Meredith's side and slid his arm around her to calm her. Braden stood beside Amy, the two of them just inside the door. He rubbed the back of his neck and shook his head at Amy as if she were upsetting Meredith deliberately.

"He did not succeed." Patting Meredith's hand, hoping to calm her, Amy added, "From now on I will be on my guard. Do not get all in a dither."

Meredith, always as sweet and cheerful as her name, squared her shoulders and clenched her fists. Despite Meredith's bout of sickness caused by the baby, Amy remembered Ian's wife had survived the frigid Alaskan winter and cared for two men, all without complaint—and certainly without climbing on a roof and crowing the sun up in the morning.

Meredith's eyes narrowed. "I am not in a dither." She turned on Ian. "What are we going to do about this?"

"Well, I thought—"

"We are going to my father's cabin and have it out with that man." Amy cut him off.

Amy shifted her gaze from Braden to Ian to Tucker. "You

know that is who pushed me. Until we prove that, no one is safe. Such a dangerous, ruthless man. He could harm anyone if his twisted mind told him to."

"Ian, you've got to see to this." Meredith wrapped her arm around Amy's shoulders.

"You don't know he did anything wrong." Braden dragged his hat off his head and hung it on the peg beside the door. "You didn't see anyone."

"We'll get to the bottom of it, honey." Ian slung an arm around Meredith.

Amy pulled away from Meredith and whirled to face Braden. "Are you going to accuse me of being a liar again?"

"We can't go off and leave the women at home." Tucker shouldered his way between Meredith and Ian. "You stay, Ian. You're a married man going to be a father. Braden and I will go to Amy's cabin and take care of this."

Braden ran both hands through his hair, his agitated motions making the unruly curls wild. He raised both hands in front of him as if surrendering. "I never said you were a liar."

"You called Amy a liar?" Meredith ducked under Tucker's arm and scowled at Braden. "Why, she's the most honest woman who ever lived."

"That is not the way I remember it, Braden Rafferty." Amy shook a finger under Braden's nose. "You accused me of—"

"Now, honey, don't go getting mad at Braden." Ian circled Tucker's huge frame and rested his hands on Meredith's shoulders.

Amy jammed her fists on her hips. "Why are we wasting time talking when we should be heading for Father's house?"

Wait on the Lord.

Amy shook her head to clear it of the impossible idea. Now was the time for action—past time in her opinion. "You are not going without me. Tucker, Braden, and I will go. Ian and

Meredith can stay here."

"I did not say you lied."

Amy glared at Braden.

"We can all go." Meredith wrung her hands as if she was afraid of being left out. "I have been in this cabin nonstop for six months."

Meredith was practically confined indoors thanks to the bear tracks Ian had seen. The only time she went outdoors was when Amy cooked their meals. And then she sat in the yard, within feet of the house. Amy knew anyone living like that would be eager for a change.

"Now, we can't do that." Ian rubbed Meredith's shoulder. "I wish we could, honey. I know you'd like to go to town."

"Are you out of your mind?" Tucker turned on Meredith. "We're not going on a picnic. You can't come. It's dangerous."

Despite the rudeness, Amy saw how dearly Tucker loved his sister.

"We are wasting time." Amy's arms flew wide. "If none of you are going, fine. I'll go myself."

"Are you out of your mind?" Braden leaned until his nose almost touched hers. "You're not going anywhere alone again as long as you live." Braden's orders only made her more impatient. "And I didn't call you a liar. I wondered if you might be mistaken is all. It's hard enough believing someone is capable of murder, but to accuse a man with no evidence—"

"The evidence—" Amy jabbed the second button on Braden's brown broadcloth shirt "—is his presence in my father's cabin. I am telling you for the last time, my father would not have sold it."

She pulled her hand back for another good jab.

Braden caught her hand. "Stop that."

Amy jerked against his grip, and he let her go.

"When you said 'for the last time,' you didn't even begin to mean it did you?" Braden sounded exhausted.

Amy clenched her fists.

"Now, Amy, you can't know that about your pa. He might have sold the cabin." Tucker hooked his thumbs into his suspenders.

"He's her father. Who would know better?" Meredith shoved Tucker sideways.

Not budging an inch, Tucker scowled at Meredith.

"And that means it was stolen." Amy ignored Tucker and jabbed Braden again. "So if my father died under unexplained circumstances, then this man is suspect in his murder."

Braden caught Amy's hand. "I told you to stop that."

"Amy's word is good enough for me, Braden. We have to help her. Stop being so stubborn." Meredith crossed her arms, the very picture of stubbornness.

"The law needs more than Amy's suspicions." Ian stuck his head between Tucker and Meredith.

Tucker quit glaring at Meredith and turned to Amy. "Don't even think of going down there by yourself."

Amy pulled against Braden's grasp.

Braden didn't let go. Fire flashed from his blue eyes.

Common sense said to give an angry man some space. She stepped closer and rose on her tiptoes. "Then you had better quit making excuses and come with me. Let us go see if the deed is still in the hidden drawer in Papa's mantel. It is just an old paper given to him by the Russian trapper who lived there before him. Father would have signed it over if he'd sold. And if the man killed my father and stole the cabin, that deed will be tucked in there, all the proof you and the law need."

Braden rolled his eyes. "We can't just go off in these woods and leave everyone behind."

"Why not?"

"It's not safe to leave Ian and Merry alone. You, Tucker, and

I would be fine, unless there's really someone after you."

Amy gasped. "You just called me a liar again." Amy whirled to face Meredith. "Did you hear that?"

Meredith stepped up to stand shoulder-to-shoulder with Amy. "I most certainly did."

"Not a liar, mistaken."

"Then we will go, just the two of us," Amy said to Braden. "We will sneak up to his place, wait until he is away, go in, and have a look in the mantel. If everything is in order, we will leave. Tucker and Ian can stay here. That way, Meredith will be safe."

"You can't sneak into a man's house," Ian pointed out. "It's against the law."

"It is not sneaking in if it is my father's house. I am welcome there."

Braden shook his head. "But you can't know if it's your father's house until after you sneak in. So it's wrong. Finding something that makes it right later still makes it wrong when you first do it."

"What are Ian and Tucker keeping me safe from?" Meredith threw her hand in the air. "Until this man attacked, I have felt as safe as a babe in arms."

"What about those bear tracks Ian saw?" Tucker reminded her.

"That was days ago," Ian said. "The bear must have moved on because the tracks are old. This isn't his regular territory. I can tell by his size he's an old fellow, and I've seen no sign of him before."

"Bears roam widely. Just because he has never been here before does not mean he is passing through," Amy said.

Ian shook his head. "He's miles from here by now, heading north. And I should be the one to go. Once we're in the wilderness, I'm the one who can find a trail and keep an eye out for trouble. And now that the bear's gone, whoever stays here will be perfectly safe."

A crash shook the cabin and startled Amy into stumbling against Braden. He wrapped his arms around her as they whirled toward the sound. The cabin door hung on one hinge, and the paw of a polar bear poked through the opening. The fierce roar of the hungry bear nearly rattled the timbers that held up the cabin.

Tucker dived for the shotgun hanging over the door. "Perfectly safe, my—"

The bear slashed at Tucker, and he stumbled back. The door tilted open at the upper left corner.

Braden grabbed Amy around the waist. He tucked her behind him. Ian caught Meredith by the shoulders and shoved her at Braden. Snagging Meredith around the waist, Braden put his body between both women and the bear. Ian ran for the door.

The bear roared. A paw slammed. The leather hinge on the bottom broke. Only the rickety wooden latch held the door closed.

Tucker, landing his back with a hard thud against the sturdy row of cedar saplings that formed the door, shoved it into place. His body and the protesting latch stood between the rest of them and a thousand pounds of enraged bear.

Tucker reached over his head, lifted the gun down off its pegs, and tossed it. Ian snagged it in midair. Braden ducked beside the door and lifted the heavy bar they dropped in place every night to secure the cabin.

Amy dashed for the bag of herbs she'd been collecting ever since she'd arrived. Thrusting her hand deep in the bag, she dug until she found the leather pouch she'd so carefully filled.

The beast barreled into the door with a vicious snarl. The door shook, and Tucker staggered forward a step. Bracing his legs, Tucker jammed the door back in place.

"When I say so, let the door go." Ian lifted the gun, keeping the barrel pointed upward over Tucker's head.

"No!" Braden shouted, lifting the massive beam. "Let's get this bar in place. It'll be enough to keep the bear out. He'll go away eventually. If we let him in, you might not get him before he hurts the women."

Amy swung the wooden shutter in the bedroom aside and poked her head out the window, looking toward the bear.

Braden caught Amy's movements out of the corner of his eye. "What are you doing?" He turned toward her.

"Scat, hintak xóodzi! Shoo, bear!" She tugged the slipknot that held the pouch closed. The bear swung its massive head at her. He fixed his beady black eyes on Amy as if he could already taste her tender flesh. The bear reared up on its hind legs. She threw the bane at the bear, pouch and all.

The pouch hit the bear full in the face and a little puff of the bitter herb dusted its snout. The growling roar cut off and turned to a whine. He retracted his claws and swiped at his face.

Braden grabbed Amy around the waist. "Get away before he—"

The bear's whining grew louder. Braden quit hollering and turned to see the animal drop on all fours and shake his head frantically, sneezing and rubbing his face on his furry foreleg. The bear looked up, and for a second, Amy stared into his eyes.

"I know it hurts, hintak xóodzi, old friend, but you should not have come here. The salmon swim thick just over the hill. Quit being lazy, and go find your own food. Leave us in peace."

Meredith shoved herself in beside Amy.

Ian stepped up behind his wife. Amy saw Tucker ease the door open an inch and peek through.

The bear seemed to be crying. Amy grinned. She knew the bitter powder would do no harm, but for a while it would sting something fierce. "Big baby."

The bear shook his head again like a dog shaking off water. Huffing, his nose and eyes streamed. Then with a wail as if he'd been soundly spanked by his mama, he turned and galloped into the woods. Amy hoped he was going fishing. The water would soothe the sting.

Meredith turned once the bear disappeared. "You have a bear repellant in your case?"

"Of course." Amy laughed. "No one lives in the midst of wolves, bears, and wolverines without a supply of it. I call it water carrot."

Tucker set the door back in place, and when it fell toward him, he dropped the bar across it with a loud clatter. "Water carrot?"

Ian stepped away from the window. "I'm really familiar with these woods. I've never heard of water carrot."

Amy shrugged. "It resembles a carrot and smells of it a bit. That may not be its true name. It is something my people use. We also call it *yán*. Before the missionaries came and told my mother's people about Jesus and the one true God, we used yán as a magic charm to ward off evil spirits."

"And bears?" Meredith asked shaking her head, still glancing nervously at the woods where the bear had disappeared.

Amy laughed. "Yes, all large dangerous animals. Now we know it is not magic; it just burns."

"And where do you find this water carrot?" Ian's brow furrowed.

Pleased Ian showed this eagerness to learn more about this new homeland of his, Amy said, "I will show you. It is dangerous though. I'm careful to never, never touch it with my bare hands. It is a deadly poison if eaten, and the juice would make you very sick if it touched your skin."

Amy thought of the plant for a second, then added, "Oh, I remember now, one of the missionaries told us yán goes by another name in the English language."

"What name?" Braden asked.

Amy carefully turned away from the group and washed her hands thoroughly as she tried to remember. "It was something about one of your ancient teachers. We studied him a bit in school." She dried her hands and turned back to the four of them, only then noticing the way they were staring at her, as if she'd wrestled the bear single-handedly rather than just tossing the bane at him. And that's when she remembered.

"Socrates." She nodded with satisfaction.

"What about him?" Meredith asked.

Ian slipped his arm around Meredith and rested his big hand on her slender waist.

"He drank the potion from this plant."

Silence stretched long in the room.

At last Meredith asked, "You mean hemlock?"

Amy snapped her fingers. "Yes, some people call it hemlock."

Ian dropped his arm from Meredith and buried his face in both hands. "Bear repellant."

"She's got hemlock in a bag." Tucker's shoulders began to tremble in a way Amy couldn't define, almost as if he were laughing. But what was funny about any of this? He ducked his head, then turned his back and went to the door. He must be preparing to mend it.

"Well, he will not be back, and it is time to fix supper. I will get smoked salmon. It will cook up quickly."

Braden rested his hands on her shoulders and turned her back to the dry sink Ian had fashioned out of a three-foot section of a hollowed-out bud gum tree. "First, before you cook our supper, why don't you wash your hands once more?"

Amy reached for the pail of water, but Braden blocked her hands and poured the water for her, then carefully wiped the bucket where she'd grasped it moments earlier. Amy let him help as she washed again, though she couldn't imagine why. Had he seen a smudge on her hands that she'd missed?

As Amy washed, Meredith came up beside her and handed her a bar of soap. "What else do you have in that bag?"

Amy accepted it and kept scrubbing. "Oh well, tundra rose, of course, and mooseberries. A bit of devil's club, although not enough. I got tired of dodging the thorns and will go back later for more. I brought in a bit of spruce tip, hard to run a home without that. And there are crushed leaves that make a wonderful mosquito repellant. We can rub it on our skin and—"

"It's not made out of nightshade, is it?" Amy noticed Meredith wringing her hands together.

"Nightshade? I have never heard of that. Does it grow around here? Does it make a good tonic?" Amy wiped her hands again on the flour-sack towel hanging on a peg near the sink. When she finished, Braden took it between two fingertips, held it far from his body, and tossed it out the window.

"How about foxglove?" Tucker kept his back to her, apparently fascinated by the door, his shoulders shaking harder now.

"Foxglove? My, no. That is not an Alaskan plant. Do you people know nothing about the northern lands?" Amy crossed her arms, wondering why they were all staring at her except Tucker, who ignored her as blatantly as the others stared.

"Wolf bane, maybe?" Ian asked. "That'd keep the mosquitoes away, I'm thinking. After all, it stands to reason that anything that'll scare off a wolf'll scare off a mosquito."

Amy frowned at them.

"Any poisonous mushrooms in that bag, Amy darlin'?" Braden shook his head at her. "Or maybe you've stored up a little rattlesnake venom?"

Suddenly they all burst out laughing.

Just as Amy's feelings began to pinch, Meredith threw her arms wide and hugged Amy until she could barely breathe.

Meredith whispered in her ear. "I'm so glad you're here."

The words and the tight hug were so sweet Amy hugged her back. She thought of Braden's arms around her on the cliff, then later when he tossed her here and there as he stood in the breach between her and a savage bear. It was a completely different kind of feeling from Meredith's hug, but he'd been trying to save her, even if it had slowed her down. It healed a lonely place in her heart to know he'd put her safety above his own.

The laughter quit hurting, and soon she joined in.

Meredith pulled away. "What in the world is a hintak xóodzi?"

"It is my people's word for the great white bear."

"Your people?" Tucker asked.

Braden and Amy exchanged a glance. Braden gave her an encouraging nod.

"Braden, you and Tucker run and fetch me the salmon. Ian, get a fire started in the fireplace. Meredith, you get comfortable at the table. I am hopeful the salmon will not upset your stomach as much as the mutton. When we are together, I will make supper while I tell you all about hintak xóodzi and my people."

fourteen

Amy wanted to march straight down to her father's cabin and confront the man who now lived there. It galled her to admit it, but she was too frightened to go alone. She didn't want to further frighten Meredith, so she didn't try to get the whole family to help her. She focused on Braden, but although two weeks had passed since the attack on the cliff, he still refused to help.

She was turning into a nag, and it was all his fault. He also wouldn't let her go anywhere alone. Amy got some satisfaction out of ordering the stubborn man around while he followed her. It neared mid-June. The days were hot, but a cool breeze kept them comfortable as Amy tramped through the woods with Braden ever watchful at her side. The snow had melted away from all but the mountain peaks.

"Pull that limb down so I can cut it." She jabbed an impatient finger at a stunted little tree with bright scarlet branches as thin as a whipcord. Amy simmered like a pot over a hot fire with the lid clamped down tight. She wanted to go to her father's, and she couldn't with Braden watching her every move.

"What are these good for?" He took notice of everything she did and helped any way she asked. This time, she was cutting tender red twigs off a dogwood tree. She respected his wish to know all about this new land. She'd been a teacher in Seattle, and it seemed natural to share her knowledge.

"I will weave a design into baskets with them." Holding up the narrow, supple twigs, she drew strength from their beauty. "The red makes a nice border design."

Satisfied with her stack of colored twigs, she went on to a stand of alder trees. Braden followed along, acting as pack mule. Amy noticed he never fully relaxed or let his attention wander from the woods around them.

"The alder bark treats infections, and I use it to tan hides." She carved slices of bark, careful to leave plenty intact so the tree would heal.

Another day, Amy pulled out the wickedly sharp knife, her only tool, and began carving. "This is a bud gum tree. Ian used a stump from one for his sink. We can also make buckets from the bark, then waterproof them with the gum. Then we will dig into the ground and steal roots. They make excellent rope."

Braden shook his head as if the bounty of nature amazed him. She climbed hills and scrambled over rocks, ignoring the ache of her hands, which still bore scrapes from her fall off the cliff. The scabs on her hands and face were mostly gone, and the skin had toughened. She hacked away at trees and shrubs without giving a thought to asking for help. He insisted on helping, of course, but she'd have let him stand by and keep watch if he hadn't offered.

She moved on to a thicket. Long yellow spines stood guard over the tender inner branches, and fragrant white flowers dotted the bushes.

Amy pulled leather gloves from her pocket and tugged them on. She had tanned the sheepskin, and cut out the fine leather to make them. "Do not help with this one. You do not want a thorn in your skin. It will fester, and it is very slow healing."

Braden caught her arm as she reached for it. "Then why don't you leave it alone?"

Amy smiled as she straightened away from the plant. "This plant does not want to share itself, but it is a plant my people prize, and we have learned our way around the stubborn thing."

"Prize for what?" The large stand of shrubs with their fierce thorns formed an impenetrable thicket that reached up the steep incline in front of them.

Amy's smile turned into laughter. "My grandmother would tell you it wards off witches and bad luck."

"Witches, huh?" Braden had set the bulk of his load on the ground, keeping his gun at hand. "Well, we don't need that since I don't believe in witches."

"Neither do I, but it makes a restorative tea, and I want some for Merry." Amy smiled. Then the smile faded. "She is getting much better, I think."

A stubborn expression came over Braden's face. "Yes, much better. This is the third morning in a row she hasn't been sick, and she stayed in the cabin while you cooked breakfast. She's still not ready to be left alone."

They'd talked of going to her father's often. Braden always had excuses why now was not the time. "She would not be alone. Ian would stay with her." Amy's eyes narrowed. "You know I need to go."

"Amy, we just can't—"

"If it were your father," she cut him off, "you would go. Do not tell me otherwise."

"It would be different in Oregon with a sheriff in town and a marshal's office to keep peace in the countryside. In Alaska, with no law closer than Dyea, the sheriff would never tramp hours into the woods after a criminal. Alaska is still a territory, and the law outside of town resembles the law in any wilderness."

Amy turned away from the nasty plant. Jerking her gloves off, she clutched them in one hand and whacked her other hand with the soft leather. "I know, and I have been patient, but it is time, Braden. We could be down there and back in one day."

Braden snorted. "The sun doesn't set. One day lasts six months."

She slapped the gloves into her hand again. "I am tired of waiting." *Slap.* "I am giving Merry a few more days." *Slap!* "Then I am going with or without you."

Braden caught the gloves, an irritated expression darkening his eyes.

"I am not going to fight the man. I am going to wait until he is gone, then slip in and out quickly." She held tight to the other end of the gloves and yanked on them.

Braden refused to let go. "You're staying right here."

"Now that I have been warned, I do not need a bodyguard." She wrenched at the gloves and stumbled forward. "I know how to move through the woods. I know the signs of others in the area. I would be fine."

One hand landed on Braden's chest, the other firmly grasped the gloves. She looked up at Braden.

He dipped his head and kissed her.

Her lips softened. Braden jumped away and turned his back.

"I have enough."

Braden turned. "What?"

"I said, I have enough. Let us go home."

"Listen, Amy." Braden caught her arm. "I'm sorry. That. . . that shouldn't have happened."

Amy turned. "You are right. And it will not happen again. I do not let men. . .close to me like that, Braden. If you would have asked, the answer would have been no."

Temper sparked in his eyes. "That wasn't only me. You kissed me back."

Amy gave his hand clamped around her upper arm a hard look. "Are you finished?"

"Yes. The afternoon is waning." Braden looked at the sky.

"The sun is going to set in, oh, about six hours, I'd say."

A tiny laugh escaped Amy's tingling lips, and she shook her head. Braden let go of her. He picked up the load she'd been gathering, and she filled the fur-lined bag she always carried, slung it over her shoulder, and filled her arms besides.

They went back toward the house together. As they neared the clearing, they saw Tucker stacking windfall branches. Meredith sat on the stump they'd used for chopping wood and sewed another shirt for Ian or one of the other men. She was keeping them all supplied with clothes.

"She is almost better, Braden."

"Just be patient, woman."

"I have been patient. More patient than any of you have a right to expect. I need to find out what happened to Papa." Amy turned and blocked the path in front of Braden. He stopped, or he'd have run over her. They faced each other with arms filled with bark and branches, leaves and roots. "Take me to my father's, or I will go alone."

Braden leaned forward until their noses almost touched, despite the load they both carried. "Fetching after your da's house is the way of a greedy woman. You have plenty here. Why do you need more?"

"I am not greedy, Braden Rafferty. This is not about that cabin. This is about justice."

"If it's not about greed, then it's about revenge."

"Justice is not revenge."

"You can't bring your father back. You can't live in that house alone. You can't even be sure someone attacked you."

"Again you call me a liar." The twigs Amy hugged to her chest snapped.

"Mistaken, not a liar. We've seen no one around. Ian, Tucker, and I are fair hands in the woods. But none of us is as good as you, are we, Amaruq Wolf Girl?"

"No, not a one of you is as good as me." She realized how boastful that sounded, and bragging wasn't what she intended. She'd merely spoken the truth.

"So, have you seen him?"

Amy raised up on her toes to shout at him before she truly thought about what he'd said. She dropped, flat-footed. "No. No, I have not seen him, nor any sign of him."

She blinked, trying to focus all her fears and finding doubts taking their place.

"Maybe that's because he doesn't exist." Braden arched one skeptical eyebrow. "Or maybe it's because some winter-crazed man like Rooster was passing through and did something cockeyed for no reason other than 'cause he's a loon."

Amy knew it wasn't true. She remembered the laughter. She'd heard it in Seattle, hadn't she? What about the menace on the *Northward* that night Braden had left her alone? What about her fear as she stood too close to the railing? It couldn't all be her imagination. She had too much respect for her instincts for that. But she was tired of wasting her breath trying to convince Braden.

"Fine, if you want to explain away what happened on that cliff, you do so. But hear this, Braden Rafferty. I am going to my papa's cabin. I am going, and I am going soon. Merry is my friend, and I will care for her as long as she needs it."

"But no longer?" Braden's eyes narrowed and anger tinged color into his freckled cheeks. "You won't turn left nor right from your obsession with your father, even if it means betraying all of us, when we took you in."

"Betraying you? You are betraying me with your doubts and insults. So no, I will not be swayed from my course."

"You're not goin' anywhere." Braden's cheeks were so crimson with anger Amy thought if she touched them her fingertips might sizzle.

"Am I a prisoner then?"

"No, there are no door locks to keep you here. But if you go, you walk away from all of us."

"By whose order? Merry would let me return. I live in her home, not yours."

"You live with the Raffertys. Do you think Ian will keep you here if I tell him I want you to leave? Do you think he'll stand by while your recklessness frightens Merry, maybe enough to make her lose their child? You already made her walk a long distance to find us when you needed help. How many times will you do that before Ian says enough?"

Amy's heart sank. Braden's words reminded her that she was indeed the outsider here. She was alone in the world. And it was for just that reason that she had to find justice for her father. She had to find the truth.

Wait on the Lord.

No! she shouted in her heart. She'd waited long enough. Too long.

"So be it, Braden. When I go, I will go for good." She whirled away and charged across the opening surrounding the cabin. She went inside and shut the cabin door before Meredith or Tucker noticed they'd returned.

❧

Braden stared at the closing door. He wanted to go in and shake her and hold her and kiss her and. . .and. . .

The ideas that came into his head shocked him, ideas of marrying Amy and having her fill up the empty places in his heart. He prayed for self-control.

Self-control. Lord, when did I start needing that?

Braden felt a weight crushing his chest as he realized Amy was in his heart. Amy was the one prompting his prayers for self-control. Amy was the one.

And she wanted to go on a long hike in the woods. Alone

with him. Just the two of them. His heart beat faster as he thought of the long hours he'd spent with her this last month and how much he'd learned and how he loved seeing her in the sunlight and twilight and any other time of day.

He took a step toward the cabin and stopped. He couldn't do it.

It would betray Maggie. Wasn't failing one woman enough? The self-control he prayed for surged to life as he realized he was forgetting the wife of his heart. The woman he'd played with as a child, held hands with as a young man, killed as a husband. God wouldn't ask him to risk another woman.

Through the window, Braden saw Amy at work over the fireplace. Amy, caring for them day and night. A true friend to Meredith. So wise in the ways of Alaska that all their lives were better for her presence.

The aroma of mutton wafted out of the cabin. Braden saw Meredith turn her head toward the scent and lose all the color from her cheeks. Clamping her hand over her mouth, Meredith jumped up. She dashed for the underbrush near the cabin and disappeared.

Tucker exchanged glances with Braden to make sure they were both aware. Braden jerked his head toward the house. Tucker nodded, hefted his Winchester over his shoulder with a quick, fluid move, and started after his sister just as the sound of retching came from the bushes.

Braden set Amy's treasures outside the cabin door when he wanted to go inside and beg her to care more for him than for her missing father. Instead, he turned his hand to collecting firewood, staying within sight of the cabin.

Protecting her from afar to protect his own foolish heart.

fifteen

"But they that wait upon the LORD shall renew their strength; they shall mount up with wings as eagles; they shall run, and not be weary; and they shall walk, and not faint."

Amy lay on her makeshift bed in the main room of Ian's cabin and read the passage of Scripture by full daylight at ten-thirty at night.

Unhappy with the message, she set her Bible down gently, resisting the urge to clap the book shut. It seemed every Bible verse she read called her to wait.

"I have waited," she whispered into the empty room. "I have been here two months now, Lord. I believe You wanted me to stay and take care of Meredith, but the summer fades quickly. I must see what happened to my father. I cannot spend a winter in comfort with the Raffertys while my father's death goes unpunished. Make a way for me to go, Lord."

Amy almost stopped before she uttered the next words of her prayer. But the need to act drove her, and she spoke quietly into the silent room. "Or I will do it on my own. You gave me a life that taught me independence. I take care of myself. I work hard. I have the skills I need, and I believe You want me to act. You are a God of justice. You do not want an evil man to hurt my papa and pay no price."

Amy lifted her Bible again, this time more tenderly, and asked God to forgive her disrespect. The book fell open, and her eyes fell on Psalm 27:14. *"Wait on the LORD: be of good courage, and he shall strengthen thine heart: wait, I say, on the LORD."*

She recalled another verse, and for the first time applied it to herself. She knew what it meant when Moses had argued with the Pharaoh to "let my people go" and the Bible said, "the Pharaoh hardened his heart."

She knew because Amy hardened her own heart at that moment. She deliberately chose a path she feared God didn't bless. Meredith was feeling better. The summer was wearing itself down. She was through waiting on the Lord or anyone else, especially Braden Rafferty.

Instead of listening to the still small voice that whispered on the wind, she made plans. Braden stayed with her nearly every minute. How could she slip away from him for long enough that he wouldn't just come after her and drag her home?

Amy sat up straight. Braden wasn't here right now. Yes, the nighttime, when she was in Ian's care, was the time to go. If someone lingered in the woods, that someone had proved to be a coward and wouldn't attack the house directly. So they'd come to expect Amy to go inside and stay. Anyone lingering in the woods wouldn't be on watch in the night.

If she slipped out as soon as the Raffertys went to bed, she'd reach her father's cabin before that horrible man got up in the morning. She'd find a hiding place, wait for him to leave, then sneak in. She'd quickly find the deed and be halfway home before the Raffertys knew she was gone.

Why, she'd even leave a note so if she didn't get back before they woke, they'd know her entire plan. And she'd meet them a few miles down the river because they were sure to come after her.

The only flaw in her plan was the worry she might cause Meredith. That was the one thing Braden said that almost swayed her. Thinking of Meredith hiking to the mine twisted Amy's stomach. Meredith could have fallen. The baby could have been lost. Amy knew she'd have to hurry to minimize

Meredith's concern. Maybe if she drove herself hard, she could be down and back before the Raffertys climbed out of bed.

Meredith wouldn't even have to cook breakfast. Amy would be home in time.

She looked out the window, considering setting off right now. But she wanted an earlier start. She'd make sure Meredith was feeling okay; then she'd go to see what had happened to her father.

Wait, I say, on the Lord.

Amy only heard the wind as she turned over and fell asleep.

ॐ

Meredith's unruly stomach had a relapse. Amy, caring for Meredith and the rest of the family, fell into bed exhausted each night for the next week. Braden was as diligent as ever guarding her—so much so that his guarding felt less like protection than like a lookout for an escape attempt. It didn't matter. Amy wasn't about to abandon Meredith. . .yet.

Amy's heart twisted when she thought of the warmth that had passed between her and Braden. It had vanished since their fight over her need to go home. Something had been lost between her and Braden. Or maybe not lost. Maybe for Braden it had never been there.

Early the next week, Meredith took a turn for the better, and Amy knew it was time to go. The first night Amy was able to stay awake long enough to hear Ian's soft snores, she tossed back the covers on her sleeping pallet and stood, fully dressed.

After tucking her knife into the sheath around her ankle, she smeared on a paste made from yarrow leaves to repel the mosquitoes. She eased the door open and closed, knowing Ian slept lightly. She stuck a note—one she'd had written for a week—on the outside of the front door.

Pulling on her walrus-gut boots, Amy strode toward the

river, listening for any sound that didn't belong in an Alaskan wilderness. As she hurried along the water's edge, she startled a porcupine and her spring babies drinking from the river. The *slap* of leaping salmon called to her as if she needed to be fishing instead of being about her father's business. When the shore allowed it, she ran, racing against the coming morning and the Raffertys' worry.

In these early days of August, the sun settled into a brief dusk, but Amy's night vision was excellent. With the moon and stars shining off the river, she found her way easily.

The river chuckled over stones. The sound soothed her agitated spirit and made her sleepy, reminding her that she'd worked a long, hard day, caring for her family.

Her family? Were the Raffertys hers? Whatever she proved about her father, she still had no one left to call her own. Meredith was like a sister to her; Ian, a protective big brother. Tucker teased Amy just as he did Meredith. Braden. . .Amy could summon no sisterly feelings for him. She'd declared that when she left, she'd leave for good. But in her heart, Amy hoped desperately that they'd welcome her back. She wanted Papa, but she wanted to belong to the Raffertys, too. Especially Braden.

Amy turned her mind away from Braden and his strong arms and the kisses they'd shared. Picking up her pace, she tuned her senses sharply toward the forest and any danger lurking there. She rushed along, setting sights for home and justice, ignoring the quiet urging in her soul to wait.

Hours later, a mile upstream of her father's cabin, she slipped away from the water and hiked into the rugged woods. The land climbed sharply upward along the riverbank, and staying under cover was hard, slow work. Her mother and father had taught her to ease her way through the woods, like smoke drifting between heaven and earth. She took great care to be silent as she pulled herself along the steep incline, hanging onto shrubs along the side of the mountain.

When her father's cabin came into sight, Amy dropped behind a large stand of cottonwood trees. She rested her head against the tree, the bark rough on her cheek. She ran her hand lovingly over the wood and remembered learning very early how to tap the cottonwood to take just a bit of the sap and then eat it fresh. These trees were the equivalent of a candy store and held precious memories for her. She looked overhead and saw the first tinge of yellow in the fluttering leaves. Already summer was slipping away. To have waited longer to see to the man who had harmed her father would be madness.

Settling in, Amy let the nature that had fed and clothed her wrap itself around her like a cloak. She heard the sharp, high cry of a raven as it swooped and dived overhead. A high, majestic scream lifted her eyes to heaven, and she saw sunlight glint off the bald head of a soaring eagle. A rustle in the bushes nearby revealed a marmot making its way to the water's edge for an early morning drink.

There was no sign of activity in the cabin. But it was too early to believe the occupant had risen for the day. An hour slipped by as she waited, and then another. Amy thought of Meredith, awake now and worrying. Amy forced herself to wait when she couldn't bring herself to before. A sound out of place with nature pulled her eyes toward the cabin. Coughing. Riveting her eyes on the front door, Amy waited, her muscles coiled, her heart thudding.

She pictured the mantel her Tlingit grandfather had carved. It had been a gift to her parents on their wedding day. The mantel carving was an intricate design in perfect harmony with the world outside the door. Grandfather had loved working with wood, and Amy had been allowed to sit by his side and watch as the beautiful creations emerged under his patient, talented hands.

He'd made her a noisy rattle and figures of animals and fish. But the mantel had been her favorite. Many endless winter days, she'd lazed in front of the fire, making up stories about the animals etched into the alder wood. She'd loved the sun and the moon. The river Grandfather carved along the bottom seemed to move when firelight flickered in the fireplace below. And the crackle of the flames passed for babbling water. Salmon were suspended, eternally leaping out of the stream, and some days Amy could almost hear them splash as they hit the water.

But most important right now was a thin drawer, its edges hidden by Grandfather's intricate carving. The drawer held the few family possessions that mattered. The deed had been ignored for the most part. Amy's father had enjoyed telling the story of the old trapper who had, with grand ceremony, presented the deed when he gave the cabin away and headed south to live out his old age with his brother.

Petrov Simonovich had never considered himself the owner of this land, so he wouldn't sell it. But if someone persuaded him to give away the cabin, he'd sign over the deed with the same pomp as the man who had handed it to him. Amy knew how to touch the carved raven and stretch her fingers wide to touch the sun, then press in on the drawer to pop it open. The deed to the property would be there.

Another cough sounded from the cabin, and Amy hunkered down a bit more. Smoke appeared in the chimney, and the smell of salmon cooking teased her nose and reminded her she hadn't eaten for hours. At last the cabin door swung open, and the man who'd driven her away from her home stepped out.

He carried a pickax over his shoulder and a shovel hanging from a pack on his back. Amy saw the man tuck a chunk of jerky into his pocket and close the door. A gust of wind carried his foul smell to Amy where she crouched twenty feet away. The man walked heavily, feet plodding along unevenly. Amy was almost certain that shuffling gait couldn't belong to the man who had pushed her off the cliff. She clenched her jaw, wondering if she'd created this whole threat out of her own fears.

He went around the side of the cabin, ragged clothes swinging their tatters in the wind. Amy remembered a game trail that led from the cabin up toward the mountaintop. He must follow it to some mine he'd found.

With a sigh of relief, Amy knew she'd have the cabin to herself. That didn't mean she'd linger. She'd grab the deed and go home. The man wouldn't even know she'd been there. Then she'd present the deed to that stubborn Braden as proof her father had met with foul play.

As Amy stood, she wondered if Braden, Ian, and Tucker would act when presented with evidence. Why had she come? Why had she ignored the urging to wait?

God, what good will it do to know my father did not sell the cabin?

The only answer she got—*wait on the Lord*—was one she refused to heed.

The miner's lumbering footsteps diminished on the path. She remembered cruel hands on her back. Saw the yawning emptiness in front of her as she hurled over the mountain's edge.

And she felt hands on her back on the *Northward* as she stood by the boat railing. Hands on her back on a busy Seattle street corner. She remembered those stealthy footfalls onboard the ship when she sat alone on the deck. Braden couldn't explain those three things away by attributing it to some person driven mad by the long, black winter. No, someone had come after her, possibly four times. She had no reason to believe he'd stop now. This had to be dealt with.

The man's footsteps faded completely. Amy squared her shoulders and ignored the internal warning that seemed to ring louder than ever. Why would God ask her to wait now? Why, when she was so close and the danger so minimal? She hurried toward the cabin.

Mindful of the way sound carried, she lifted the heavy front door, hinged with worn leather, to keep it from scratching as she swung it open. Leaving it barely wide enough to slip through, Amy headed straight for the mantel. There was no reason to stay a second longer than necessary.

Amy reached her left hand for the precious raven and the sun that glowed in the bright sheen of aged wood.

The wicked laugh she'd heard twice before rumbled behind her.

Hands shoved her into the mantel.

Amy's chest slammed into her grandfather's intricate carving. She staggered sideways, caught her balance, and whirled around.

≈

Braden still battled the long daylight hours. He had adjusted somewhat, but he'd wake up to full light and have no idea whether it was 1:00 a.m. or high noon. As a result, he'd learned to roll out of bed quickly, feeling late.

He pulled on his clothes. His belly told him it was breakfast time even if the sun wouldn't cooperate. Maybe Ma did the right thing, packing that fancy clock. Leaving the cabin, he walked down the path to Tucker's, looking for a clearing overhead that would give him a good look at the sun. He still stung from the ribbing Tucker and Ian had given him the time he'd awakened Tucker just one hour after they'd gone to bed.

Finding a likely spot, Braden studied the sky and decided it was a wee bit early. He'd go on to Ian's, gather wood for a while, and leave Tucker sleeping for another hour. As soon as he stepped into the clearing by Ian's cabin, he saw the white paper fluttering on the front door. Braden rushed forward and pulled the note free.

> *I have gone to get proof of what happened to my father. Do not worry about me. I will be back in time for breakfast.*
>
> *Amy*

Braden stared at the note, fury riding him as he thought of the headstrong, impetuous woman. She might meet up with whomever wished her ill. The ache in his heart at the thought of losing Amy forever nearly drove him to his knees.

"Ian, wake up!" Braden hammered on the front door with the side of his fist, regretting that Amy's reckless behavior was going to put all of them in jeopardy.

Ian opened the door in his bare feet and long underwear.

Braden shoved the note into his hand. "You can't leave Merry. I'm going after Amy."

Meredith appeared in the door, peeking over Ian's broad shoulders.

"Get Tucker first," Ian said. "I don't want you out there alone."

Braden shook his head. "No time." He turned toward the river.

"Braden!" Ian's voice stopped him.

He turned back.

Ian reached over his head and pulled down the Winchester. He thrust it at Braden. "Wear those boots, too. They're waterproof." Ian jerked his chin at the boots that lay on the ground. Braden realized there'd been four pairs lying there last night. Now there were three.

"I don't want to leave Merry home alone. We'll go for Tucker together. He'll be after you as soon as he can get on the trail."

Braden jerked the boots on and ran for all he was worth toward the river. He glanced over his shoulder to see Ian and Meredith walking swiftly toward Tucker's cabin in their nightclothes, Ian's arm protectively wrapped around Meredith's waist.

Braden charged down the rocky beach. When the creek bank grew too steep, he'd weave into the shallow water, his feet splashing, his lungs heaving as he pushed himself. The gun hung heavy in his grip as his arms swung in time to his long-legged pace. The voice of God pushed him as surely as if the wind had hands. And the cry of the raven shouted for him to *hurry, hurry, hurry*.

sixteen

Amy looked into the shifty eyes of Barnabas Stucky.

"Well, if it isn't the pretty little lady from the boat." Stucky's clothes, new on the boat, now hung off him like filthy rags. The smell of him nearly made her retch. His hands with broken, dirt-caked nails, reached for her, and she backed away until her shoulders were pressed against the mantel.

"You've been a hard one. But you're not gettin' away this time."

The look of pure cruelty on his face spurred Amy to action. She grabbed for the knife in her ankle sheath. Stucky's hands closed on her wrist before she could reach it. He dragged her forward, shoving her into a chair so hard it knocked the wind out of her. Jerking at his belt, he pulled it free and bound her hands in front with the coarse leather.

"Who are you?" Amy's heart hammered in her chest. Why hadn't she waited?

"My brother sent me to find you when he got this cabin. He knew you were the only one on earth who'd complain."

"Complain? Because Papa sold out?" Amy's stomach sank, knowing the truth without the man speaking another word.

"No, 'cause your pa refused to sell out. Here's your plumb stupid old man sittin' on gold that'll make the Klondike Gold Rush look like a little pile of granite. Your father owned it all and didn't even know it was there. When Owen found the gold, he took the claim. This is a land for the strong, and your father was an old, weak man."

"That is a lie. My father was getting older, but he was still a strong man. The only way your brother could have hurt him is to shoot him in the back or push him off a cliff."

Barnabas was close enough that she could smell his fetid breath. His teeth, yellow and broken, were bared at her in a savage mockery of a smile. "Reckon that's what he done."

"So, your brother is a coward just like you," Amy taunted. "He would never take on a strong man face-to-face when you are too afraid to face a woman half your size." Amy thought of her knife. If she could goad him into releasing her, perhaps to prove his courage, she could win any fight they had.

Barnabas laughed and tightened the belt around her hands. "Once Owen got to the cabin, he found all your letters and the daguerreotype you sent your pa. He wanted to make sure you never found your way home."

"And he knew just the snake that would do his dirty work, didn't he?" Amy strained under the leather binding as she spat the words at her captor.

Barnabas laughed. "Owen knew I was fresh out of Yuma prison and needin' money. I wouldn't have had to come all the way here if that wagon had done you in on the streets of Seattle."

"You almost pushed me off the boat." Amy shuddered at the man's twisted smile. The full beard he'd grown, only stubble on the boat, made him look more animal than man.

Stucky's eyes, as cold and dark as an Alaskan January, narrowed. "I lost you at Skaguay. Figured you'd go all the way to Dyea and weren't payin' attention. That's the only reason it took me as long as it did. Then I came home after you went over the cliff. I never dreamed you came out o' that fall alive."

He bent down until his face was level with hers. "You're a hard one made for a hard land, ain'tcha, missy? Well, I'm a hard one myself. My brother finally let me move in with him onest you was dead. He's gonna pay me cash money to clear his rights to this holding."

Amy lunged for his throat with her bound hands. With a crude, growling laugh, Stucky blocked her, snagging the belt that held her hands. Amy kicked at him, landing a hard blow to his ankle that knocked one of his feet out from under him. He fell forward. Amy jumped from the chair. Stucky lunged at her and sank his fingers into her long braid. He jerked, slamming her back on the chair.

"You want to fight? We'll fight." Stucky grabbed Amy by the throat. His powerful grip tipped the chair backward as he stood and fumbled for a leather strap hanging over the mantel.

Amy clawed at his hand, fighting for breath. Clumsily, he bound one leg to the chair, then the other. Once she was pinned down, he wrapped a longer strap around her waist. Panting from the exertion, he moved away from her.

Completely immobilized, Amy saw the rage in Stucky's eyes and knew she had to talk fast if she wanted to live. So far, Barnabas Stucky had shown interest in only one thing. "How much is he paying you? I could pay you more."

Stucky laughed. "A hundred dollars. And don't think you can trick me. I already checked in Seattle to find out how much money you had. People have bought their way out of trouble with me before. You didn't have enough to beat Owen's offer." He laughed and curled his fingers into claws, then reached for her throat.

"One hundred dollars? While he gets my gold mine?" Amy nearly stumbled over her words. "You saved it for him. You deserve half that mine. If you helped me get it back, I would give you the whole thing."

Stucky stopped short, his hands extended. The calculating look returned to his eyes, this time layered with something other than cruelty. Greed.

"You'd never hand over this claim. I know better than that. But my brother should be payin' me more. If he's gonna be a rich man while I'm doing all the dirty work, then I deserve to be his partner." Stucky's high-pitched laughter filled the room again.

Amy heard the nervous mania that was so evident in all the stampeders. If he would just go, she might be able to get to her knife, then free herself and get away.

Oh God, forgive me. Forgive my impatience. If only I had waited.

"If Owen wants me to clear the title to this land, he's gonna have ta pay." Stucky checked Amy's bonds, then gripped her chin and lifted her face. "I'll be back, li'l Amy. Nothin's gonna change for you, but it is for me. You're gonna make me rich."

Laughing, he turned and raced out of the cabin.

The second Barnabas vanished, Amy struggled to reach her ankle. The tie at her waist kept her from bending. Her leg wouldn't rise. Minutes ticked by as she fought the leathers; they only tightened. She had no idea how far Barnabas would have to walk to find his brother. With a near howl of frustration, she pulled her hands to her mouth and began chewing on the brown, tough leather of Stucky's belt. As the minutes turned to an hour with only a bit of headway on her bonds, she fought down panic, knowing he couldn't be gone much longer.

The door flew open, and Braden charged inside, his leveled Winchester sweeping the room.

"Braden," Amy choked, losing a battle against tears.

"Are you alone?"

"Yes, there are two men, both of them gone. But they will be back. We have got to get out of here!"

"I'll be right back."

Amy wanted to scream at him not to leave. She fought

down the impulse. She knew Braden well enough to know he wasn't about to abandon her.

Braden checked the bedroom Amy's father had built for her.

Amy sighed with relief when he came back out.

"No one here." He drew his knife from his belt. With a slash, he freed Amy's hands, then made quick work of the rest of her bonds.

He helped her from the chair. "We've gotta get out of here before they come back. We'll get you home. Then Ian, Tucker, and I will come and settle this." Braden tried to slide his arm around her waist, but she stepped away.

"Let me get my father's deed first. It will only take a second."

"It can wait, Amy. We've got to get clear of this place."

"He admitted that the man who lived here killed my father." A renewed spate of tears shook her body.

Braden's jaw tensed. "Make it quick."

She turned toward the mantel.

"We won't let him get away with it. I'm sorry we didn't come here sooner and find out what happened."

Amy reached for the raven and sun. "No, it is my fault. God has been telling me right along to be patient, to let Him set the time for justice. But I did not listen. And you put yourself in danger because of my stubbornness. I should have waited for help. I am so sorry." Her tears blinded her as she fumbled with the stiff wooden levers.

Braden rested one hand on her trembling shoulder. His strength helped ease her tears.

"This is the first time you've ever admitted you were wrong."

Amy glanced over her shoulder, glad for his teasing tone that steadied her. "That is because this is the first time I have been wrong."

Braden coughed, then laughed out loud. "And it's the first

time you've ever said you needed help."

Amy looked up at him and opened her mouth.

Braden laid one finger on her parted lips. "Don't say it. I know. You've never needed help before, either."

Amy shrugged and felt sheepish because that's exactly what she'd been planning to say. "Let me get the deed. Then we will get away from here. He will be gone a while, I expect, but I do not want to take a chance."

Braden jerked his chin in agreement. Amy reached for the carved mantel again just as heavy footsteps sounded on the path behind the house.

"They are coming." Amy started for the front door.

Braden grabbed her by the wrist. "Too late!"

seventeen

Braden raced for the back room, dragging Amy along. He swung the door open, lifting so it made almost no sound. Amy held her breath as the two men's voices grew closer.

Once in the back room, she ducked behind Braden, who swung the door shut and turned to face it. Amy sensed Braden's rigid attention to every sound outside the door. He lifted his rifle so it pointed toward the ceiling, his thumb on the hammer, his finger on the trigger.

The men were arguing as they strode down the trail.

"You'll pay up or you'll kill her yourself."

Amy heard Stucky's vicious, heartless discussion of her life and death reduced to a matter of dollars and gold dust.

"I ain't gettin' my hands dirty killin' a pretty little woman in a territory where there's only about ten of 'em," Stucky continued. "Not for a measly hundred dollars. An ole trapper disappears—nobody thinks too much of it. A young woman living with a solid family like the Raffertys goes missin', and questions'll be asked sure as certain."

"I'm not givin' you half this claim," Owen raged. A hard fist pounded on the outside door. "I'll up the price to two hundred dollars, but that's highway robbery. We made a deal. And no one knows you're here. No one's gonna blame you for nothing."

Owen's voice sent chills down Amy's spine. This man had killed her father. This man had hired a man to murder her. All for gold. Now he bartered for her life with less emotion than most people would show buying a bolt of cloth.

Braden watched through a crack between the saplings bound together to make the door. He took a second to look away and gave her a nod of encouragement. His eyes, sharp and intelligent, told her he'd protect her with his life. She stood behind him, her left shoulder pressed against the wall like his. The fingers of his right hand steady on his rifle, he reached behind with his left and caught her hand, lacing his fingers together with hers.

Amy had never felt more connected to another human being. Braden offered her protection, using his body to shield her. She tightened her grip on his hand as his strength drove the chill away.

"Thank you," Amy whispered. She pulled her hand free of Braden's so he'd be able to move quickly.

The door to the cabin swung open.

"She's gone!" Stucky's voice mixed with shouting from Owen.

"You said you'd tied her up." Owen's fury cut through the room. "We've got to find her."

Amy froze. The walls weren't that solid, and movement could possibly be seen through cracks. Any creaking wood, even just from shifting weight, might draw the men's attention to this room. She saw Braden's shoulders tense beneath his brown shirt and didn't realize what he meant to do until he'd moved.

Swinging the door open, Braden stepped into the main room. "Put up your hands."

Gun level, his voice bitter cold, he froze the two men in their tracks.

Amy peeked around Braden's broad shoulders. Neither man had a gun. She could see that now. Braden must have noticed this fact and decided to end the nightmare right here.

"Both of you sit down." Braden gestured with the muzzle of

his gun toward the two chairs in the room. One of them still had leather straps hanging from where Amy had sat bound.

"What are you doing in my house?" Owen backed away, looking between Braden's eyes and the gun. "This is trespassing. I'll have you arrested."

"This is one of them Raffertys," Stucky said.

Owen cut him off. "He don't have no proof 'a nothin'." Owen scowled at his brother, then slumped into a chair.

Amy slipped out of the back room and stood behind Braden.

Both men's eyes widened. Barnabas Stucky's face turned beet red, and Owen bared his teeth until Amy expected him to growl. The two men looked alike now that she saw them together. Middling tall, stout of build, dark hair streaked gray, full shaggy beards—in that they looked like most of the men who came north. But they also shared ruthless blue eyes and cruel lips. Hate etched the same lines into their faces.

Braden held them captive, but now what did they do?

As if she'd asked the question aloud, Braden said, "Stay behind me." He planted himself between the front door and the two snarling men with Amy at his back. "Tucker's on the way. We'll hold 'em here 'til he comes, then go on into Skaguay and leave them with the sheriff."

"We ain't done nothin' wrong." Owen erupted from his chair.

Braden leveled the rifle. Amy couldn't see Braden's expression, but she saw Owen blanch and sit back down.

"Whatever you want here, mister, just take it," Owen sputtered. "I'm a law-abidin' man. I don't know what you're talking about, takin' us to the sheriff. There's no call—"

"You killed my father." Amy stepped up beside Braden, her temper too hot to think of safety. "You have tried to kill me four times."

"He's tried four times?" Braden glanced at her, his brow furrowed. Then he went back to watching his prisoners.

Amy nodded and pointed at Stucky. "He admitted it. On his brother's orders, he tried to kill me in Seattle, then twice again on the boat. He never caught me alone for long enough."

She looked at Owen. "So do not waste your breath with lies. Braden came in and found me tied up, and we heard what you said to your brother when the two of you came back to the cabin. It is not my word against yours. Braden is a witness, too. You cannot explain that away."

"Hey, whatever my brother did ain't no business o' mine." Owen glared at his brother.

Stucky's jaw tightened. Fury burned in the man's eyes until Amy thought he'd attack Owen. She realized that unless they could break Owen's story, Barnabas, who had tried to kill her but never managed it, might be arrested. Owen, the man who had murdered her father, might go free.

Before Barnabas could accuse his brother, a noise caught their attention from behind. Amy whirled around and looked into the eyes of Darnell Thompson, the other man who'd paid so much attention to her on the boat. He held a Colt revolver in his hand, pointed steadily at Braden's midsection.

Braden's finger tightened on the trigger. Amy prayed, knowing her recklessness had brought Braden to this moment. She might be responsible for his death.

"Ease off, Mr. Rafferty. I'm not here for you. I'm here for him." The gun shifted from Braden to Owen. "I've been hunting you for a long, long time. I lost your brother's trail in Dyea, and it's taken me a long while to get here. But this is the end of the line for you and your claim jumpin' ways."

Thompson, dressed like a stampeder with three-months growth of beard and a probing, assessing look in his eyes, reached into the pocket of his brown wool pants and pulled out a badge. "I'm a Pinkerton. If you even remember anymore, you killed a man in Texas nearly four years ago and sold off his homestead. You prey on men who live alone, far from anyone. But this Texan had friends. He was a loner, but his father is a powerful man back East who kept track of him quietly. When his son came up missing, he called in the Pinkertons."

"So you have proof he is a thief and a murderer?" Amy stepped sideways to let Thompson inside.

"I followed Stucky north, hoping he'd lead me to his brother. I saw Stucky gettin' ready to shove you over the railing of the *Northward*."

Amy's eyes widened in shock. "You saw him? Why did you not arrest him?"

"I saw what was in his eyes, miss," Thompson said. "The evil intentions he had toward you. But he didn't do anything because I stepped in with that trumped-up story about wanting to come with you. I was just makin' talk until your watchdog got there."

"Watchdog?" Amy's forehead wrinkled.

"Rafferty. I saw him coming your way, and when he got close enough so Barnabas couldn't hurt you, I eased back. Another reason I didn't accuse him of anything was because I wanted him to lead me to his brother. Now, I'm taking Owen back to Texas to stand trial. And I reckon we'll just throw Barnabas right on in with him."

"But what about my father?" Amy looked between Thompson and Braden. "How does a jail cell in Texas add up to justice for Papa?"

"A noose, when it comes, collects all a man's debts." Thompson tugged the front of his Stetson low on his forehead. "He'll pay for it all, miss. Don't you worry. I'd like you to write a letter explaining all that happened here for me to take back. He's done this a heap of times and left a trail of death across this country. But this is the first time he's ever stayed put long enough for me to catch up with him. He'd kill the landowner, sell the property as his own, and then move on. Not sure why he stayed here."

"I know why." Amy nodded. "This is the first time he has ever found gold."

"It's mine. No one is going to take it from me." Owen lunged out of his chair at Amy.

Braden grabbed his shoulder and sat him down hard.

"We'll just have your word for this theft because there's no proof your father's dead without a body. Some old trappers keep moving. But your testimony will add weight to the charges."

"I can do better than write a letter. I can prove he stole this land."

Thompson gave her a long, sharp look.

Braden smiled encouragement at her.

She carefully skirted the two outlaws and went to the mantel.

Touching the sun and the raven at the same time with her left hand, she pressed in on the hidden drawer until she felt the catch snap. Sliding the drawer open, she stared down at the old deed, yellow with age. She slid the papers out carefully and gently unfolded the brittle document. This was the last thing connecting her to her father. Tears burned her eyes as she thought of the gruff but loving man who'd brought joy to her childhood and whom she'd missed terribly all her years in Washington. She'd never see him again.

Turning, she took the deed to Thompson. They looked down and saw that the land title was unreadable.

"What is that?" Braden glanced at the papers but went back to watching Owen and Barnabas. Amy noticed Thompson's watchful eyes only looked away from the men a second at a time, too.

"It is in Russian." Amy's voice faded. She swallowed and continued. "I had forgotten. I always knew the drawer was there and what it contained, but we did not get it out often. Probably not since I was too young to read."

"That isn't a deed. It's chicken scratchin's that prove nothin'," Owen raged. "And some man comes in here and says he's a lawman." Owen glared at Thompson. "He don't have any say over me up here in the Alaska Territory."

"You won't be in the Alaska Territory for long." Thompson pulled shackles from the pack he carried on his back. Thompson gave one last grim look at the deed. "Too bad that's in Russian. To have solid evidence in Alaska would strengthen my case in Texas. Don't reckon there'll be anyone between here and there that'll read Russian."

Amy's heart ached when she thought of her father and all she'd lost. "He killed the only man I knew who could read it."

"He's covered his tracks with killing for years."

"This time he picked a man who didn't kill so easy." The deep voice filled the cabin.

They all whirled around.

Petrov Simonovich stepped into the cabin.

"Father!" Amy launched herself at the thin figure who had replaced the robust man who'd raised her. She'd take him however he looked.

Her father caught her to him with a soft grunt. "My Amy." His arms wrapped around her with a strong grip that belied his slender frame. "You've come home."

Amy heard a crash and turned to see Owen running toward the small cabin window. Thompson dove for him and dragged the killer to the ground before he could escape. Barnabas jumped at Braden, who'd lifted his gun off the prisoners when Amy had distracted him.

Amy's father set her aside, reached for the man grappling

for the gun, and hurled him against the solid wood mantel with a dull thud.

Braden took one look at Barnabas as he crumpled unconscious to the floor, then turned to Thompson. "Let him up. I've got you covered."

"Yep, 'n' if you don't, I do." Petrov chuckled.

Braden gave Petrov a narrow-eyed look.

Petrov clapped Braden on the back. "Sorry, boy. I know you're doin' fine." He turned back to Amy and pulled her firmly into his arms.

"They told me you were dead, Papa."

Petrov grunted. "Not the first time nor the last they'll prove up to bein' stupid."

Amy smiled and clutched her father tight, afraid to believe her own eyes. "Where have you been all this time? You stopped writing months ago."

"That one there"—Petrov nodded at Owen as Thompson pulled him to his feet—"shoved me over a cliff last winter, clear up north of here, broke my leg in the fall. He stood over me and laughed about leaving my body for wolves."

Amy turned and pulled back her leg to give Owen a swift kick.

Her father stopped her, laughing, and hugged her again. "Always was a feisty one, my Amy."

Amy saw Braden nod and heard him whisper to Thompson, "That's the honest truth."

Amy's father looked over her shoulder for a long time. Amy pulled back far enough to know he was staring at Braden. A firm jerk of her father's chin seemed to settle something between him and Braden. Then Papa set her on her feet and reached for the deed, which had fallen to the floor.

"I'll do more than translate this for you. I'll go with you back to Texas and make sure he stands trial for all he done to me."

"But Father, what about me? I want you to stay here in this cabin with me."

"I'll be back." Amy's father turned to her. "You're in good hands here with your young man."

"He is not my young man." Amy glanced over her shoulder at Braden.

Braden grinned. "Sure I am."

Braden lowered his rifle now that the Stucky brothers were securely shackled. He came forward, his hand extended. "Petrov Simonovich, I'm Braden Rafferty. And I'd be proud to take care of your daughter, sir."

"I—I cannot live with Ian and Merry any longer," Amy stuttered.

Amy watched Papa shake hands with Braden as if they were sealing a bargain.

"No, you can't." Braden released her father's hand and took hold of hers. "That'd never be fittin' for a married woman."

"A what?" Amy's jaw went slack.

"Her mother was like this, too, son." Petrov chuckled again. His full beard quivered. Amy remembered his broad, deep-chested strength.

"But Father, what happened to you after Owen shoved you?"

"Now's not the time for that. You need to talk to your young man."

"Tell me!"

Papa and Braden exchanged a long look. Her father shook his head and sighed. "I got taken in by your mother's people. They found me before the wolves did, but they were on their way to their winter hunting grounds and didn't have time to bring me back. My leg was mighty slow in healing. Looked for a time like I might lose it. One of your mother's uncles seemed way too willin' to be the one handling the knife when the time came. It was a powerful incentive to keep on healing up."

"But still, why would it take you so long to get back? Summer is nearly over. You could not have been healing all this time."

A high-pitched wail came from outside the cabin.

"Come on in. It's safe."

A woman, dark and quiet with the serene eyes Amy remembered from her mother, came into the cabin, carrying a baby.

"We had to wait until my son was old enough to travel." Petrov smiled.

"Son?" Amy saw two little fists reach up from a blanket woven of fine goat hair. She leaned against Braden without thinking about it. He wrapped his arm around her waist and pulled her close.

"Amy, this is my wife *Guwakaan*."

"Deer, what a beautiful name." Amy left Braden's side and rested a hand on the petite lady, quite a bit older than Amy but still a young woman, svelte and graceful as a deer. She could give her father many sons and daughters yet.

Amy had to smile, thinking about her father with little ones around his knees. He'd been a wonderful father to her, and he'd been alone for a long time. This would make his life rich again.

"And we called the baby *Ch'ak'yéis'*," Petrov nodded with a look so proud Amy thought the laces on his buckskin shirt would burst.

"Young Eagle. Perfect," Amy said.

"I s'pose." Her father frowned. "I wanted to name him Boris."

Guwakaan looked up. She'd been demurely shining her midnight eyes on her son, but now she smiled at Amy and rolled her eyes. Amy had to fight to hold back a laugh. She knew she and Guwakaan would be good friends.

"Are you interested in a trip to Texas, Guwakaan?" Amy asked.

"I will go where Xóots leads. I would enjoy seeing more of this great land."

"Xóots? You call my father grizzly bear?" Amy giggled.

Guwakaan nodded. "But he is a skinny bear these days. He lost too much weight healing, then more growling because the healing was slow. I will fatten him up." Despite her teasing, she turned adoring eyes on Amy's father, and he pulled her into a gentle hug that included the baby.

Amy remembered her mother using the same tone when she talked about her father. This one would make Father very happy.

"Uh, Mr. Simons?" Braden squared his shoulders.

"It's Simonovich, son. Done with all that passin' for anything I ain't. Proud of my Russian blood."

"Good, what I was going to say is, uh. . .you're rich, sir. Aye, you've got yourself a gold mine. And if these two speak the truth, it's a good one."

Guwakaan spoke quietly. "We cannot eat góon. I can see it if it makes a good spear tip or a pot, but why the madness around the góon?"

Petrov said to Braden, "You take it, son. I've found plenty of ways to dig a living out of this frozen world. I don't need a bunch of yellow rock to make me happy."

Braden shook his head. "I'm finding enough of my own. Just traces, nothing big, but that suits me. I hate the thought of another gold rush, this one aiming straight at me. I think I'll just leave it for you. Maybe someday Ch'ak'yéis' will want the gold."

"We will raise him better than that, Xóots. Just wait and see." Guwakaan and Amy's father exchanged a look that spoke of complete agreement.

"So when do we head for Texas?" Petrov looked at Thompson.

Amy's stomach sank when she thought of her father leaving. Then she remembered what Braden had said about getting married.

"Right after the wedding." Braden turned to Thompson. "You're a lawman, closest thing we've got around here to a judge. You can speak some vows."

"True enough," Thompson said. "I'm sworn to do such things by the state of Texas. I'm not sure if it's okay up here, but no one will care."

"Well, I certainly care!" Meredith stepped into the cabin, her hands on her hips, her cheeks flushed. "You'll be married by a proper minister, and that's that."

"What is going on here?" Ian asked.

Tucker stood behind him.

Braden gave them a shortened version. The nearest minister was in Skaguay. Thompson, the Stucky brothers, Petrov, Guwakaan, and Ch'ak'yéis' were all heading that way anyway. So it was decided the Raffertys, Tucker, and Amy would accompany them, have the wedding, and return home together after seeing Amy's father off.

Meredith acted as if she'd been given a priceless gift when they decided she could go.

Amy stood listening to them, her temper growing until she thought her insides would explode. She opened her mouth to tell them all their planning was for nothing because someone had yet to properly propose.

Wait on the Lord.

Amy froze. If she'd waited, her father would have handled these men, then written and sent for her. If she'd waited, she wouldn't have risked her life on that cliff when Barnabas pushed her. If she'd waited, she wouldn't have been at the mercy of Barnabas Stucky. Had she learned nothing?

She calmed down and turned to Braden.

He smiled at her. "I think we've forgotten something mighty important, haven't we, little Amaruq?" He took her arm and led her out of the cabin. With a backward glance he said, "And you all give us a few moments of peace while I ask this woman to marry me."

Her calm turned to serenity as Braden pulled her to stand beneath a cottonwood turning to blazing yellow. The leaves fluttered overhead like the wings of angels. A raven swooped low and called out. The river rustled and bubbled nearby as it rushed toward Skaguay. She and Braden would soon rush along with the river toward Skaguay, too, because of course she was going to say yes, if he ever got around to asking.

Braden wrapped her in his arms.

She waited for the sweet words of love every woman longs to hear.

"When I realized you'd run off this morning, I wanted to wring your neck."

Amy lowered her expectations considerably. So Braden didn't have the Irish gift for sweet blarney. So he didn't possess that poetic Irish soul she'd heard tell of. So he was a lunkhead. So what? It didn't matter. She loved him.

Braden brushed her hair off her forehead and leaned close. "I knew if something happened to you my life would never be the same. And I'd have to live with the knowledge that my unwillingness to help you with something so dear to your heart might have cost your life."

"Oh, Braden, it would not have been your fault. God told me as clear as the call of a raven that I needed to wait. He has been trying to slow me down since I decided to climb on that steamship and come hunting my father. If I had left everything to God, all would have worked out. My father would have handled Owen and Stucky. Thompson would have shown up to take the men back to Texas just as he did today without me in the way causing trouble. Then Papa would have stopped in Seattle to see me, and I would have come home.

"It was all my fault. I want to charge in and do everything, but God wants me to learn to wait. He wants me to learn patience. From now on, I am going to listen to God's voice and wait on His timing. I understand how this land works. I have always waited for spring to come again with no desire to force my own ideas about light and dark, winter and summer. I have learned now that I need to do that in everything."

"Uh. . .can you wait right now?"

Amy tilted her head. "Wait for what?"

"For me to get a word in edgewise. I want you to marry me, Amy. I love you. And if you'd waited, we'd have never met."

"Yes, we would have. I would have come home with Papa on his way home from Texas. You would have been my nearest neighbor. Oh yes, we would have met because God wants us to be together."

Braden nodded.

Amy had to speak of the one worry that plagued her heart. "And if I had waited, you would have had the time you needed to grieve for your beloved wife. In that, too, I did damage, forcing you to compare me to your graceful, ladylike wife with my crude mountain ways."

"Stop." Braden laid his hand gently on her mouth. "Is that the way it seemed to you?" Braden pulled her tightly into his arms. "Forgive me, Amy. It's true that my grieving hadn't run itself dry. But all I felt was guilt and anger, not sadness. You even got me past that."

"Guilt?" Amy pushed away from him far enough to look in his eyes. "Why would you feel guilt for your wife's death?"

"Maggie was never strong. Having a baby was very hard on

her. She was not cut out for life on the frontier and I knew that. But I couldn't imagine living in the city. If it hadn't been for me, she'd have gone back East. She had a chance because she had an aunt back there who would have taken her in. But I loved her, and she wanted to stay with me. I wanted to have a family. Every way I looked at it, she seemed to have died because of me, and I couldn't forget her dying in my arms, crying for me to save her. I left home, feeling like a failure."

"But Braden—"

Braden shook his head. "Let me finish."

Amy waited.

"I know now there is no sense in those thoughts. The Lord giveth. The Lord taketh away. God gives no man the strength to save a life if God wants to bring one of His children home. When I compared you to Maggie, my guilt came because I found Maggie so lacking. Maggie never would have stepped in and cared for the family like you did. She'd have complained and handed off every job there was to someone else. I loved her and cherished her, but she wasn't fit for the rugged life we live. You are perfect for it. Perfect for me. She was the love of my youth, and I'll always cherish her. But you are the love of my life."

A smile spread across Braden's face. "You're the one God wants me to spend my life with. I know that as surely as I know the sun will rise in the morning." Braden looked up at the always-light sky. "Okay, I really don't know if the sun will rise in the morning anymore."

Amy patted him on the chest. "You will get onto the ways of Alaska in time."

"I will. I love you and want you to marry me." Braden kissed her lightly on the cheek. "What do you say, lass? Are you going to wait this time? Or is this one time you can plunge right in?"

Amy smiled, then laughed and looked up at the wide,

glorious sky, the towering pines, the soaring eagles, and the shining sun. "I do not hear God saying to wait. Not for this."

He kissed her again. She didn't wait an instant before she kissed him back.

epilogue

They made it to Skaguay in time to lock the Stucky brothers in the town jail to await the next steamer and their ride back to Texas and justice.

Meredith tried to talk Amy into buying a new dress, but the prices horrified Amy.

"I prefer sheepskin anyway, Merry. Why would I spend money like this for a dress made out of thin calico that won't last?"

Meredith fussed at her, but Amy wouldn't be budged.

Braden left the women to shop for other things while he found a preacher.

Parson Henderson had come to bring God to thousands of madmen and admitted he found his work trying. He insisted on spending the day with them.

Braden and Amy were married in front of a tent—Parson Henderson's church. Amy's father and his wife and son were there, along with the Raffertys and Tucker.

Guwakaan had gathered a bouquet of yarrow and daisies for Amy. Amy held them easily, surprised by the strong assurance from God that she and Braden were meant to join their lives.

Pastor Henderson, a gaunt man, tall and gangly but with a serene smile that reflected his devotion to God, spoke the vows.

"Do you, Braden—"

"Pastor Henderson, excuse me, but can I make my own promises to Amy?" Braden interrupted.

Looking surprised, Pastor Henderson said, "Of course, if the vows are made to Amy before God."

"They are." Braden turned to her and took her hands in his. He smiled gently, and Amy's heart became his without a word spoken.

"Your hands are callused." He held them snugly as if trying to warm them.

"I am sorry." Was this when he remembered his fine, gentle wife?

"I love that about you." Braden cradled her hands against his chest.

Amy's doubts faded away under the shining light in his eyes.

"I love that you are strong. I love that you know this land and respect it and understand it. I think I loved you from that first day I sat beside you on the boat, but I was too afraid to trust my heart and the voice of God telling me He'd led me straight to you. You are going to be a source of strength for me all our lives."

"You do not need my strength, Braden. You saved my life. You were there, helping me on that cliff and at Papa's house because of your strength and wisdom and your caring spirit."

"Although I have my own strength, I need yours as well," Braden said. "Having a real partner to stand beside will make us more than we are alone. I promise before God to always love you, always honor you, and always cherish you."

"And I promise before God to love, honor, and cherish you, too, Braden."

"And obey?" The twinkling light in Braden's eyes made it easy.

"Yes, I'll obey you. Because I know you will not ask anything of me that is not right. And I know you will listen to me."

Braden nodded. "And I know that if you object to something I say, it will be for a good reason. I'll listen to that reason, and we'll decide what's best together."

Amy whispered, "Amen."

"Amen." Braden kissed her.

Pastor Henderson blessed their vows.

Amy kept expecting that warning voice to tell her, *Wait*. It never came.

She and Braden had waited until this golden day, until God's own time. They'd waited long enough.

A Letter To Our Readers

Dear Reader:
In order that we might better contribute to your reading
enjoyment, we would appreciate your taking a few minutes
to respond to the following questions. We welcome your
comments and read each form and letter we receive. When
completed, please return to the following:

Fiction Editor
Heartsong Presents
PO Box 719
Uhrichsville, Ohio 44683

1. Did you enjoy reading *Golden Days* by Mary Connealy?
   ❑ Very much! I would like to see more books by this author!
   ❑ Moderately. I would have enjoyed it more if

   _____

   _____

   _____

2. Are you a member of **Heartsong Presents**? ❑ Yes ❑ No
   If no, where did you purchase this book? _____

   _____

3. How would you rate, on a scale from 1 (poor) to 5 (superior),
   the cover design? _____

4. On a scale from 1 (poor) to 10 (superior), please rate the
   following elements.

   ____ Heroine   ____ Plot
   ____ Hero   ____ Inspirational theme
   ____ Setting   ____ Secondary characters

5. These characters were special because? _____
   _____
   _____

6. How has this book inspired your life? _____
   _____
   _____

7. What settings would you like to see covered in future
   Heartsong Presents books? _____
   _____
   _____

8. What are some inspirational themes you would like to see
   treated in future books? _____
   _____
   _____

9. Would you be interested in reading other **Heartsong
   Presents** titles? ❏ Yes ❏ No

10. Please check your age range:
    ❏ Under 18   ❏ 18-24
    ❏ 25-34   ❏ 35-45
    ❏ 46-55   ❏ Over 55

Name _____
Occupation _____
Address _____
City, State, Zip _____

Petticoat Ranch

Lose yourself in this rollicking adventure-packed romance about a headstrong mountain man and an independent frontier woman who butt heads and tangle hearts in Texas.

A delightful romance by award-winning author Mary Connealy.

Historical, paperback, 288 pages, 5³/₁₆" x 8"

Please send me ____ copies of *Petticoat Ranch.* I am enclosing $6.97 for each.
(Please add $3.00 to cover postage and handling per order. OH add 7% tax.
If outside the U.S. please call 740-922-7280 for shipping charges.)

Name_____

Address _____

City, State, Zip _____

To place a credit card order, call 1-740-922-7280.
Send to: Heartsong Presents Readers' Service, PO Box 721, Uhrichsville, OH 44683

Hearts♥ng

HISTORICAL ROMANCE IS CHEAPER BY THE DOZEN!

Any 12 Heartsong Presents titles for only $27.00*

Buy any assortment of twelve *Heartsong Presents* titles and save 25% off of the already discounted price of $2.97 each!

*plus $3.00 shipping and handling per order and sales tax where applicable. If outside the U.S. please call 740-922-7280 for shipping charges.

HEARTSONG PRESENTS TITLES AVAILABLE NOW:

___HP480 *Sonoran Star*, N. J. Farrier
___HP483 *Forever Is Not Long Enough*, B. Youree
___HP484 *The Heart Knows*, E. Bonner
___HP488 *Sonoran Sweetheart*, N. J. Farrier
___HP491 *An Unexpected Surprise*, R. Dow
___HP495 *With Healing in His Wings*, S. Krueger
___HP496 *Meet Me with a Promise*, J. A. Grote
___HP500 *Great Southland Gold*, M. Hawkins
___HP503 *Sonoran Secret*, N. J. Farrier
___HP507 *Trunk of Surprises*, D. Hunt
___HP511 *To Walk in Sunshine*, S. Laity
___HP512 *Precious Burdens*, C. M. Hake
___HP515 *Love Almost Lost*, I. B. Brand
___HP519 *Red River Bride*, C. Coble
___HP520 *The Flame Within*, P. Griffin
___HP523 *Raining Fire*, L. A. Coleman
___HP524 *Laney's Kiss*, T. V. Bateman
___HP531 *Lizzie*, L. Ford
___HP535 *Viking Honor*, D. Mindrup
___HP536 *Emily's Place*, T. V. Bateman
___HP539 *Two Hearts Wait*, F. Chrisman
___HP540 *Double Exposure*, S. Laity
___HP543 *Cora*, M. Colvin
___HP544 *A Light Among Shadows*, T. H. Murray
___HP547 *Maryelle*, L. Ford
___HP551 *Healing Heart*, R. Druten
___HP552 *The Vicar's Daughter*, K. Comeaux
___HP555 *But For Grace*, T. V. Bateman
___HP556 *Red Hills Stranger*, M. G. Chapman
___HP559 *Banjo's New Song*, R. Dow
___HP560 *Heart Appearances*, P. Griffin
___HP563 *Redeemed Hearts*, C. M. Hake
___HP567 *Summer Dream*, M. H. Flinkman

___HP568 *Loveswept*, T. H. Murray
___HP571 *Bayou Fever*, K. Y'Barbo
___HP575 *Kelly's Chance*, W. E. Brunstetter
___HP576 *Letters from the Enemy*, S. M. Warren
___HP579 *Grace*, L. Ford
___HP580 *Land of Promise*, C. Cox
___HP583 *Ramshackle Rose*, C. M. Hake
___HP584 *His Brother's Castoff*, L. N. Dooley
___HP587 *Lilly's Dream*, P. Darty
___HP588 *Torey's Prayer*, T. V. Bateman
___HP591 *Eliza*, M. Colvin
___HP592 *Refining Fire*, C. Cox
___HP599 *Double Deception*, L. Nelson Dooley
___HP600 *The Restoration*, C. M. Hake
___HP603 *A Whale of a Marriage*, D. Hunt
___HP604 *Irene*, L. Ford
___HP607 *Protecting Amy*, S. P. Davis
___HP608 *The Engagement*, K. Comeaux
___HP611 *Faithful Traitor*, J. Stengl
___HP612 *Michaela's Choice*, L. Harris
___HP615 *Gerda's Lawman*, L. N. Dooley
___HP616 *The Lady and the Cad*, T. H. Murray
___HP619 *Everlasting Hope*, T. V. Bateman
___HP620 *Basket of Secrets*, D. Hunt
___HP623 *A Place Called Home*, J. L. Barton
___HP624 *One Chance in a Million*, C. M. Hake
___HP627 *He Loves Me, He Loves Me Not*, R. Druten
___HP628 *Silent Heart*, B. Youree
___HP631 *Second Chance*, T. V. Bateman
___HP632 *Road to Forgiveness*, C. Cox
___HP635 *Hogtied*, L. A. Coleman
___HP636 *Renegade Husband*, D. Mills
___HP639 *Love's Denial*, T. H. Murray
___HP640 *Taking a Chance*, K. E. Hake

(If ordering from this page, please remember to include it with the order form.)

Presents

___HP643 *Escape to Sanctuary*, M. J. Conner
___HP644 *Making Amends*, J. L. Barton
___HP647 *Remember Me*, K. Comeaux
___HP648 *Last Chance*, C. M. Hake
___HP651 *Against the Tide*, R. Druten
___HP652 *A Love So Tender*, T. V. Batman
___HP655 *The Way Home*, M. Chapman
___HP656 *Pirate's Prize*, L. N. Dooley
___HP659 *Bayou Beginnings*, K. M. Y'Barbo
___HP660 *Hearts Twice Met*, F. Chrisman
___HP663 *Journeys*, T. H. Murray
___HP664 *Chance Adventure*, K. E. Hake
___HP667 *Sagebrush Christmas*, B. L. Etchison
___HP668 *Duel Love*, B. Youree
___HP671 *Sooner or Later*, V. McDonough
___HP672 *Chance of a Lifetime*, K. E. Hake
___HP675 *Bayou Secrets*, K. M. Y'Barbo
___HP676 *Beside Still Waters*, T. V. Bateman
___HP679 *Rose Kelly*, J. Spaeth
___HP680 *Rebecca's Heart*, L. Harris
___HP683 *A Gentlemen's Kiss*, K. Comeaux
___HP684 *Copper Sunrise*, C. Cox
___HP687 *The Ruse*, T. H. Murray
___HP688 *A Handful of Flowers*, C. M. Hake
___HP691 *Bayou Dreams*, K. M. Y'Barbo
___HP692 *The Oregon Escort*, S. P. Davis

___HP695 *Into the Deep*, L. Bliss
___HP696 *Bridal Veil*, C. M. Hake
___HP699 *Bittersweet Remembrance*, G. Fields
___HP700 *Where the River Flows*, I. Brand
___HP703 *Moving the Mountain*, Y. Lehman
___HP704 *No Buttons or Beaux*, C. M. Hake
___HP707 *Mariah's Hope*, M. J. Conner
___HP708 *The Prisoner's Wife*, S. P. Davis
___HP711 *A Gentle Fragrance*, P. Griffin
___HP712 *Spoke of Love*, C. M. Hake
___HP715 *Vera's Turn for Love*, T. H. Murray
___HP716 *Spinning Out of Control*, V. McDonough
___HP719 *Weaving A Future*, S. P. Davis
___HP720 *Bridge Across The Sea*, P. Griffin
___HP723 *Adam's Bride*, L. Harris
___HP724 *A Daughter's Quest*, L. N. Dooley
___HP727 *Wyoming Hoofbeats*, S. P. Davis
___HP728 *A Place of Her Own*, L. A. Coleman
___HP731 *The Bounty Hunter and the Bride*, V. McDonough
___HP732 *Lonely in Longtree*, J. Stengl
___HP735 *Deborah*, M. Colvin
___HP736 *A Time to Plant*, K. E. Hake
___HP739 *The Castaway's Bride*, S. P. Davis
___HP740 *Golden Dawn*, C. M. Hake

Great Inspirational Romance at a Great Price!

Heartsong Presents books are inspirational romances in
contemporary and historical settings, designed to give you an
enjoyable, spirit-lifting reading experience. You can choose
wonderfully written titles from some of today's best authors like
Peggy Darty, Sally Laity, DiAnn Mills, Colleen L. Reece,
Debra White Smith, and many others.

When ordering quantities less than twelve, above titles are $2.97 each.
Not all titles may be available at time of order.

SEND TO: **Heartsong Presents** Reader's Service
               P.O. Box 721, Uhrichsville, Ohio 44683
Please send me the items checked above. I am enclosing $ _____
(please add $3.00 to cover postage per order. OH add 7% tax. NJ
add 6%). Send check or money order, no cash or C.O.D.s, please.
To place a credit card order, call 1-740-922-7280.

NAME _____

ADDRESS _____

CITY/STATE _____ ZIP_____

HPS 5-07

♡

HEARTSONG
PRESENTS

If you love Christian romance...

$10.⁹⁹

You'll love Heartsong Presents' inspiring and faith-filled romances by today's very best Christian authors. . .DiAnn Mills, Wanda E. Brunstetter, and Yvonne Lehman, to mention a few!

When you join Heartsong Presents, you'll enjoy four brand-new, mass market, 176-page books—two contemporary and two historical—that will build you up in your faith when you discover God's role in every relationship you read about!

Mass Market 176 Pages

Imagine. . .four new romances every four weeks—with men and women like you who long to meet the one God has chosen as the love of their lives…all for the low price of $10.99 postpaid.

To join, simply visit www.heartsong presents.com or complete the coupon below and mail it to the address provided.

✂ -

YES! Sign me up for Heart♥ng!

NEW MEMBERSHIPS WILL BE SHIPPED IMMEDIATELY!
Send no money now. We'll bill you only $10.99 postpaid with your first shipment of four books. Or for faster action, call 1-740-922-7280.

NAME _____

ADDRESS_____

CITY_____ STATE _____ ZIP _____

MAIL TO: HEARTSONG PRESENTS, P.O. Box 721, Uhrichsville, Ohio 44683
or sign up at WWW.HEARTSONGPRESENTS.COM